A

CANDLELIGHT REGENCY SPECIAL

Candlelight Regencies

216 A GIFT OF VIOLETS, *Janette Radcliffe*
221 THE RAVEN SISTERS, *Dorothy Mack*
225 THE SUBSTITUTE BRIDE, *Dorothy Mack*
227 A HEART TOO PROUD, *Laura London*
232 THE CAPTIVE BRIDE, *Lucy Phillips Stewart*
239 THE DANCING DOLL, *Janet Louise Roberts*
240 MY LADY MISCHIEF, *Janet Louise Roberts*
245 LA CASA DORADA, *Janet Louise Roberts*
246 THE GOLDEN THISTLE, *Janet Louise Roberts*
247 THE FIRST WALTZ, *Janet Louise Roberts*
248 THE CARDROSS LUCK, *Janet Louise Roberts*
250 THE LADY ROTHSCHILD, *Samantha Lester*
251 BRIDE OF CHANCE, *Lucy Phillips Stewart*
253 THE IMPOSSIBLE WARD, *Dorothy Mack*
255 THE BAD BARON'S DAUGHTER, *Laura London*
257 THE CHEVALIER'S LADY, *Betty Hale Hyatt*
263 MOONLIGHT MIST, *Laura London*
501 THE SCANDALOUS SEASON, *Nina Pykare*
505 THE BARTERED BRIDE, *Anne Hillary*
512 BRIDE OF TORQUAY, *Lucy Phillips Stewart*
515 MANNER OF A LADY, *Cilla Whitmore*
521 LOVE'S CAPTIVE, *Samantha Lester*
527 KITTY, *Jennie Tremaine*
530 BRIDE OF A STRANGER, *Lucy Phillips Stewart*
537 HIS LORDSHIP'S LANDLADY, *Cilla Whitmore*
542 DAISY, *Jennie Tremaine*
543 THE SLEEPING HEIRESS, *Phyllis Taylor Pianka*
548 LOVE IN DISGUISE, *Nina Pykare*
549 THE RUNAWAY HEIRESS, *Lillian Cheatham*
554 A MAN OF HER CHOOSING, *Nina Pykare*
555 PASSING FANCY, *Mary Linn Roby*
570 THOMASINA, *Jean Vincent*
571 SENSIBLE CECILY, *Margaret Summerville*
572 DOUBLE FOLLY, *Marnie Ellingson*
573 POLLY, *Jennie Tremaine*
578 THE MISMATCHED LOVERS, *Anne Hillary*
579 UNWILLING BRIDE, *Marnie Ellingson*
580 INFAMOUS ISABELLE, *Margaret Summerville*
581 THE DAZZLED HEART, *Nina Pykare*

JESSICA WINDOM

MARNIE ELLINGSON

A CANDLELIGHT REGENCY SPECIAL

Published by
Dell Publishing Co., Inc.
1 Dag Hammarskjold Plaza
New York, New York 10017

Copyright © 1980 by Marnie Ellingson

All rights reserved. No part of this book may be reproduced or transmitted in any form or by any means, electronic or mechanical, including photocopying, recording or by any information storage and retrieval system, without the written permission of the Publisher, except where permitted by law.

Dell ® TM 681510, Dell Publishing Co., Inc.

ISBN: 0-440-14633-X

Printed in the United States of America
First printing—July 1980

JESSICA WINDOM

Chapter One

The Viscount Markham sat staring at the flames in his lately deceased neighbor's grate and cursing his bad luck at having timed his visit home so poorly. Another week in London and he would have missed the funeral, and more importantly, this interminable condolence call on which his mama, the dowager viscountess, had appealed to him to accompany her.

He had not seriously objected to attending the funeral. It was his duty after all, and the vicar was too sensible a man to try to make an overly mournful occasion out of the loss of one who, the viscount believed, would not be sorely missed. However, when his mama begged his company on this visit to the bereaved family, he should have been quick enough to invent a pressing engagement elsewhere.

This feminine gibble-gabble threatened to continue forever, and purely feminine it was, for Harry Broyles, only son and heir of the late departed, was racketing about in Ireland somewhere, no doubt on the lookout for horseflesh, and his exact whereabouts had not yet been discovered.

"Isn't it just like Frances to do a bolt before Monty

was even underground?" the late Mr. Broyles's sister spoke, her narrow face made still more severe by the pursing of her lips.

"It wasn't precisely a bolt, Aunt Chudleigh," the plump young woman at her right said. "Cousin Frances merely announced her intention of leaving to take up residence with her old friend in Torquay. And what does it matter, after all? Harry won't want a hostess here. He'll doubtless marry soon now that he's come into the property."

"Yes, Elvira's right," the younger of Harry's two sisters spoke up. "The only job for Cousin Frances to do here now that Papa's gone would be to chaperone Jessie, and that won't be necessary, for I've decided to take her to live with me. She'll like looking after dear little George and Annabel."

Her aunt sniffed. "*You've* decided, Nerissa? And since when have family decisions been given to you to make? I am going to give poor Jessie a home."

Nerissa's small dark eyes flashed angrily. "That should be pleasant for her, waiting on your mama-in-law hand and foot."

Mrs. Chudleigh's skin took on a mottled look. She stared balefully at her niece's smart black crepe with the cut-jet buttons. "Pleasant! Much you care about pleasing Jessie. You want to be able to turn off your nanny so that her wages can go onto your back instead of into her pocket. You were ever one to squeeze a penny except when it came to decking yourself out."

Nerissa's chin jutted out. "Well, if we're going to talk of being clutch-fisted, if you and Uncle Chudleigh didn't find it cheaper to live with his mother, you wouldn't have to worry about someone to fetch and carry for that tiresome old lady."

"Tiresome? She's a most genteel person. Jessie will enjoy playing cards with her occasionally and having some adult conversation. I daresay it will be a great treat compared to chasing after your offspring—who are, and I say it to your face, extremely spoiled."

"Perhaps Jessie has a preference," Lady Markham said gently, interrupting this exceedingly vulgar exchange. "Have you, dear?"

The subject of the conversation, though the participants had spoken as if she were not present, was indeed among them, though sitting so quietly on a low stool gazing into the fire that it was difficult to believe she had been following the suggestions pertaining to her destiny.

She was a little dab of a thing, no more than two inches above five feet, and the hastily contrived mourning dress, which had obviously belonged originally to someone of stouter frame, gave her the appearance of a child playing at dress-up. Her dark curls were awkwardly cropped and gave her an untidy, urchin appearance.

And indeed, orphan she was, some connection of the late Monty Broyles, whom he had fetched from heaven knew where when she was three years old, to become his ward.

Mr. Broyles had not been much given to generous impulses, and in point of fact his generosity in this case did not seem to have stretched so very far, the viscount reflected. True, he had given the child a roof over her head, but apparently not much else. Lord

Markham was certain she had been treated as a general slavey by the Broyles offspring, whom she called cousin, though perhaps the connection was not so close as that. Even the roof he had provided was a very ugly one. Gray Gables, the house was called, and as unprepossessing a heap of stone as one could find, inside and out.

It seemed to have been arranged with a total disregard for comfort, much less elegance. That hideous side table, for instance, which the viscount had spent some moments staring at in morbid fascination. If a table with an apron in the shape of a goat's head and legs that tapered down to cloven hoofs had ever been fashionable, that day was long past. Anyone who cared for his surroundings would have relegated it to the lumber room long since. Even the fire here in the drawing room did not seem to give off much heat, but perhaps it was just that Gray Gables was too drafty to keep out the February chill.

The girl Jessie, at being addressed by Lady Markham, now turned from the fire. She had a round face with a well-shaped mouth, but her nose was far from elegant. It was straight enough but a shade too sharp and could best be described as pert. She turned clear gray eyes on Lady Markham.

"Preference?" she repeated. "No, I haven't a preference for either position. I shouldn't like to waste my education."

For a moment the room was so quiet that even the fire seemed to have stopped crackling. Then Elvira let out her breath in a long, disapproving, "*Well.* When my sister and my aunt have been so kind as to offer you a home! How grieved my poor papa would be to hear you so ungrateful after he kindly burdened himself with your keep all these years. And now when his family shows willingness to do the same—"

"It isn't necessary for them to do so," the child said. "And it wouldn't be a challenge. Your children are too young to need a governess, Nerissa, and I can't think that Aunt Chudleigh's mother-in-law has the least need of anyone beyond a sort of servant-companion. I don't propose to waste my education playing at piquet and winding wool. It—it would be quite wicked. I shall get a position teaching in a school."

This astonishing revelation silenced them all again, and the viscount's attention was fairly caught. The child had spirit, which resounded strongly through the soft, well-modulated words.

"A *school*! And what school do you think would hire *you*, miss?" Mrs. Chudleigh asked angrily.

"I should think a great many. You see, the one thing of real value that your brother gave me was an education."

"Lessons from the vicar!" Elvira scoffed.

"Yes, and lucky it was for me that your papa was too—that he chose not to hire a governess. He offered the vicar a few shillings a week to teach me my letters. And later when I was old enough to have been sent to a second-rate girls' school, the vicar offered to keep me on. Your papa was glad to save the money. And that was my great good fortune, for Mr. Raynes is a most learned man, and I daresay I learned ten times more from him than I would done from any governess your papa would have hired or any school he would have sent me to. I can teach French, Italian, Latin, and I'm fairly proficient in Greek. And from Lady Sarah I learned to sing and play the pianoforte and harp. Oh, and I *can* teach watercolor painting, though unless one has a great deal of talent, that does seem a pallid pursuit, don't you think?"

As her stunned audience made no comment, she considered thoughtfully, then amended, "Though I suppose it is useful for sketching one's specimens on botanizing expeditions, after all. It is only rocky eminences and lonely fir trees that are so trivial when poorly done."

Lady Markham was the first to find her voice. "My dear child, you sound most accomplished, but you are so very young."

"I'm very nearly eighteen," the girl offered.

"There; you see? At seventeen you would be no older than some of your pupils."

Jessie gave a small sigh. "Yes, I should like to have been a *bit* older before searching for a position. In fact I'm afraid that my Cousin Broyles's death was somewhat untimely."

The viscount choked.

"However," Jessie went on, "I could seek a post as governess for a year or two, but *not* in a house where the children are so very young."

"Nor so very old either," Lady Markham said.

Jessie considered this. "Yes, I suppose a young lady of sixteen or seventeen might not like to take discipline from me."

Markham met his mother's eyes with wry amusement in his own, as he knew she had not been thinking about daughters who were too old, but sons who might very well make cakes of themselves over Jessie. In most households with sons of a certain age, a governess such as Jessie would be most unwelcome. She was certainly no beauty, but she was a taking little thing with those great dark-fringed gray eyes and the air of self-assurance which was so much at variance with her innocent urchin-child look.

"Dear me," he said. "This does present a problem. A position must be found with children not so old as to be likely to flout Miss Jessie's authority, but not too young to bore her. If they wish to learn Latin, Greek, and the harp, so much the better."

Jessie's cousins laughed spitefully, but she merely turned a bland countenance to him. He had the oddest feeling that the lack of expression was a carefully schooled response that hid some emotion she did not wish to display—anger, hurt, or possibly contempt for one who would speak so thoughtlessly of what must be, to her, a most pressing matter and lay her open to her relatives' ridicule. But she only said mildly, "Very true, Lord Markham, but it is not your problem, after all."

At these words uttered in a tone so devoid of reproof, he realized with a stab of annoyance that it was his problem after all. By his rank and standing as the major landholder and only peer in the neighborhood, he must assume some responsibility for this waif. Her late guardian's estate was a minor one, indeed he was so careless of his acres that Markham had often been annoyed to see the waste, but he must have made it pay after all, for there always seemed money enough to improve his stables, his son Harry was indulged in every way, and his daughters had been sent to London for their come-outs with all the proper accouterments for securing husbands. But it would be surprising indeed if Broyles had done anything for his ward in his will. After the astonishing act of establishing her at Gray Gables, he had apparently ceased to notice her. The viscount had seen her from time to time, shabbily dressed and always alone, trudging the long miles into the village. Occasionally he had caught sight of her in his meadows (on botanizing expeditions?), and once or twice he had spied her in boy's trousers riding astride one of Broyles's cobs in the back lanes. The first time this had happened she couldn't have been more than ten and he himself about twenty. She had looked so alarmed at seeing him that he had called out reassuringly, "Don't worry, I won't tell." He had thought at the time that it was a shame that with Broyles's large stable, his ward was not being taught to ride properly, for she handled the horse well, though it was large for her.

Yes, she had been neglected during her guardian's life and would doubtless be the same at his death, but at least these grasping harpies must not be allowed to use her as unpaid labor. Of course she was ridiculously young to think of going out unprotected into the world, but—

He looked at his mother with a lift of the eyebrows. "Eugenia?" he said softly.

She considered, then shrugged. "It might serve." And then addressing Jessie, "My dear, there is a possibility—a possibility only, mind you—that my daughter,

Lady Harewood, might need a governess. Her elder daughter, Claire, has been in a girls' seminary in Chelsea but contracted a rheumatic fever and had to be sent home. She is recovered but very frail and cannot return to school for the rest of the year. Delphina, the younger daughter, is only five. I believe her mother was on the point of hiring a governess for her, but Claire's illness upset the household rather badly. But now that Claire is able to resume her studies, my daughter is in need of a governess, most assuredly. Would you like me to write and ask if she has engaged anyone yet? Besides the two girls, there are only the boys, who are younger than Claire and have their own tutor. They will present no problems at this time, I feel very sure," she said with a humorous look at her son.

"Or perhaps you think a five-year-old is beneath your notice," the viscount said impulsively, and immediately wished the words unsaid.

"Not at all," the girl said with complete composure. "The first years of schooling are vitally important. It is merely that it would be a waste for me to serve as a nanny to infants too young to learn their letters. To be a good nanny one need only be sensible and warmhearted."

"Well, no one would ever accuse Jessie of that," Nerissa said, sniffing. "Deserting the family that has given her her keep all these years—kept her out of the workhouse where she belonged!"

"Perhaps I did belong there, but your papa claimed me as a relation. I believe it is not at all unusual for a gentleman of substance to shelter his more unfortunate relations." There was a fine flush on the girl's high cheekbones, but she spoke without heat. "And in the last years I think I have earned my keep. I have done all the household mending since I was eleven years old, as both Cousin Frances and the housekeeper are too shortsighted to do it properly. And when your papa and brother invited parties down for the shooting season, who do you think took care of all the details—the flowers, the silver, the extra baking? Surely you must know there aren't servants enough in the household to manage."

Nerissa was very red in the face, the red of anger rather than embarrassment, and she said with curling lip, "I'm sure these simple tasks must have given you great pain, being so far beneath your touch—you with your brilliant mind. It's odd that none of us ever noticed your brilliance until you so kindly pointed it out to us."

"I never claimed to be brilliant," Jessie said with dignity, "but I was schooled by a learned man—who taught me for a pittance out of his own goodness of heart. It would be a waste of all his work if I didn't make use of his teachings."

"Then it's settled," Lady Markham said firmly before any more wrangling could ensue. "I will write to Lady Harewood."

"If you please, ma'am," Jessie said. "I will write down my qualifications for you." She rose quickly and went over and seated herself at a writing table.

The viscount listened to his mother, amused and impressed, as she kept up a flow of perfectly correct and polite conversation for all the world as if none of the unpleasantness of the last half-hour had occurred.

In a short time Jessie was back. Lord Markham rose and took the sheet of paper to hand to his mother. He glanced at the beautiful hand in which the list of her proficiencies was inscribed. With some surprise he saw that she had signed it "Jessica Windom."

"Jessica Windom?" he said. "I had thought your name was Jessie Broyles."

"Well, it is *not* Broyles," she said, and for the first time he sensed a little crack in her composure. "My cousin said—he was quite clear on that point. My name is Jessica—" and there was a fraction of a second's hesitation "—Jessica Windom."

Chapter Two

Lady Sarah Raynes, the vicar's wife, was the daughter of an earl and might have looked as high as she pleased for a husband, but in her first London season none of the advantageous offers she had received awoke even a tremor of response in her heart, and in her second season she had tumbled head over ears in love with Matthew Raynes. He was the younger son of a country gentleman and destined for orders. Though his father lacked a title, his bloodline was as respectable as that of the earl himself, and seeing that Sarah had quite made up her mind, her family gave consent to the marriage.

It had been a singularly happy one. The Reverend Mr. Matthew Raynes might have had a more splendid preferment had he wished, but he had been Staffordshire born and bred and had sorely missed the country when he was away from it. From his viewpoint the church of St. Cuthbert's at Littledene had everything to recommend it. Littledene was the prettiest village imaginable, surrounded by a number of small estates belonging to country gentlemen of solid worth. It was located in the heart of the country he loved and only a half-day's journey from his wife's family's seat. His closest friend from Oxford days lived only some forty miles distant, making frequent visits possible, and it was not so far from London but what he and his wife could journey thence once or twice a year whenever they chose to avail themselves of the amenities the city had to offer.

Lady Sarah's constitution, though far from sickly, was a trifle delicate, and the country air and quiet life suited her to perfection. She had a warm heart and was a great favorite with her husband's parishioners.

Their only son, Edward, had just gone up to school when Monty Broyles had approached Mr. Raynes about giving lessons to his ward. A vainer man would have been insulted at Broyles's assumption that the vicar would leap at the opportunity of earning the pittance he offered. Mr. Raynes's income was quite adequate to his standard of living, and he valued his free time, which he spent in scholarly pursuits. But he was not a vain man, so he took no insult, but rather took pity on the poor child in Monty Broyles's care and agreed to the arrangement.

He had had no cause to regret the impulse, for young Jessie surprisingly proved to be an excellent student, devouring lessons as eagerly as another child might devour a plate of cream buns.

As for Lady Sarah, being for the first time in so many years without her own child in the house, she had fallen victim at once to the wistful appeal in the girl's great speaking eyes and had discovered with delight that underneath Jessie's sober appearance lay not only a heart starved for love but a first-rate mind with a comical twist of humor.

She had opened her heart to Jessie, or Jessica, as she soon desired to be called, and the child had responded with an outpouring of affection for both of her mentors. Lady Sarah thought it remarkable that anyone coming from the dour Gray Gables and the careless tyranny of the older Broyles girls could find anything to laugh about, but laugh she did, and the vicarage was a merrier place for it.

Once, thinking to offer Jessica a treat, Lady Sarah had proposed taking her on a visit to her brother's home and had been surprised to see the flicker of joy in her eyes at once quenched by fear.

"Oh, no, ma'am. Please do not suggest such a thing to my cousin!" And seeing Lady Sarah's bewilderment, Jessica had added, "You see, it would be such a mark of particularity, and that would not serve. You have never done such a thing for Nerissa or Elvira."

Lady Sarah could scarcely repress a shudder at the notion of bearing either of the older Broyles girls' company for more than a half-hour. In Christian charity she would show them courtesy and render them any aid possible in time of trouble, but their conversations were so tedious and self-centered, and their characters so vulgar, that nothing would induce her to spend more time in their company than the neighborly dictates of propriety suggested.

"You see," Jessica said, "it would make them envious, and that would not at all be the thing!"

Lady Sarah's heart was wrung at the realization that this child had had to learn so young that she must

21

hide what she valued or it would be taken from her by her odious family, for that was surely what frightened her. Her place in the affections of her friends here at the vicarage, her love of learning, her quickness of mind—did she have to wear them all secretly, as she did her little locket, under her clothing safe from jealous eyes?

She and Matthew would do all they could to make her lot easier, if love could accomplish it, and if hiding their affection from Jessica's family would serve that end, then they would do that too.

Now on a dark afternoon a fortnight after Monty Broyles's funeral, the maid announced Miss Windom.

"Jessica, my dear, come in. I can see by your face that there is news." Lady Sarah came forward to greet her young friend and drew her into the vicarage drawing room. "Come closer to the fire. The day is so raw."

Jessica held her hands to the inviting blaze, but her eyes were on the older woman's face. "Lady Harewood says she will be pleased to have me. I'm to go as soon as it can be arranged."

"Well, this is good news, is it not? I knew Lady Harewood when she was a girl, and I feel sure she will be a kind employer. She was a bit of a scamp in those days, so I daresay she will not be at all stiff." And then, seeing the faintest shadow in the girl's eyes, she slipped an arm around her shoulders. "Of course you know how very much we shall miss you, and if there should be anything you cannot like in your situation, you must come back to us at once and we will

22

start afresh. Indeed, nothing would please me more than to have you with us always—"

"But it would not serve, you know, ma'am. Mrs. Edward cannot like me, and she is such a good daughter-in-law in every way, besides having given you quite a *passable* grandson."

Lady Sarah chuckled reprovingly at this sally, for it was well known that she positively doted on her grandchild, who was indeed a splendid little fellow.

"And it would be so uncomfortable if she were to find me actually living here that she would not visit half as often as you would wish."

"Yes, it is most vexing. Why cannot all our acquaintance behave just as we would like?"

"I can understand how it is with her," Jessica said dispassionately. "And I am a good deal to blame. When she first came here as your new daughter, she was almost a stranger, and yet she found me, with no claim on you at all, running tame about the house almost as if I belonged."

"And so you do, love."

"But it was tactless of me to let her see how at home I felt here. What makes it particularly stupid is that I was always so careful at Gray Gables never to let them know how attached I was to you and Mr. Raynes. And I blush to remember that when Mrs. Edward came, I made a pun in Latin, showing off, and she didn't understand it but the two of you laughed. No wonder she never forgave me. And having taken me in aversion, it could only become worse, since I'm an orphan. I'm sure she feels very keenly that one *ought* to like orphans, and since she could not like me, it must have made her feel very guilty. It's no wonder she can hardly bear the sight of me."

Lady Sarah's soft voice disclaimed, "I'm sure it's not as desperate a case as that. And anyway, she's safely off in Dorset at the moment, and you will always be a welcome guest in this house. So you must promise to let us know if all is not well with you at the Harewoods'."

Jessica gazed into the face of her dear friend. "I will indeed." Then her serious look vanished and she opened a parcel. "Now tell me, do you think this braid is sober enough to trim my gray dress? Cousin Frances turned out an old trunk of hers when she was packing for Torquay and gave me quite a few bits and pieces as well as a length of really nice wine-colored kerseymere. She never has done such a thing before in all the years I have known her. What would you think of this lace to edge a fichu?"

The two settled down contentedly in front of the fire to talk of clothes.

At Ashendene Lady Markham kept country hours, except when her son was in residence. Tonight he finished his port and joined her in the library. She put her book aside at once. He sat on the opposite side of the fireplace, and when he didn't speak, she repeated several bits of neighborhood news she had gleaned during a morning call. He listened attentively, and yet he seemed somewhat abstracted.

"Robert, I know you had a good deal of estate business to look into when you came down to Ashendene, but—was I wrong, or did you have something you wanted to talk to me about as well?"

If he was surprised it showed in no more than a brief flare of light in his eyes. "I always like talking to you, love."

"I see." She picked up her embroidery and studied it thoughtfully. "I just thought there might have been something special."

"And what special thing did you imagine it to be?"

"Oh, I conjectured you might be going to tell me you had offered for Carolyn Warriner," she said in an offhand way.

His eyes narrowed in alarm. "Don't tell me that one of your cronies has reported I've been so particular in my attentions to her that people are talking!"

"No, darling, I'm sure you've been most circumspect and would not raise false hopes if you didn't intend to offer. It's only that my Cousin Edwina wrote me that you had put Miss Warriner's brother's name up at White's and that he's a callow lad who still has spots. She took it as a sign."

"Good God, Mama!"

"Well, Edwina was ever one to add six and six and come out with fifteen."

"To tell the truth, I did have it in mind to speak to you about Carolyn."

"Oh?" she said carefully. "She's a pretty-behaved girl and her family is unexceptionable—except for her brother's spots. You have decided, then?"

He sank his chin into his hand. "No, the devil of it is, as the days have passed, it's occurred to me that absence hasn't made my heart grow fonder. Perhaps I'm not cut out to be married."

"That's your decision, of course, Robert."

He looked at her with a wry smile. "No, Mama, stop humoring me. It's time for you to remind me that I have a duty to my name."

"One thing I've never had to remind you of is your duty, dearest. Sometimes I think you remember your duties all too well. Perhaps if you ignored some of them you would be less—bored?"

"Is that what I'm feeling, Mama? Boredom? Yes, I suppose my reluctance to come to the point with Carolyn is because the thought of being married makes me feel—bored. I wonder why that should be?"

"I should think because you haven't fallen in love with her."

"Oh, *love*," he said, dismissing it with a wave of his hand. "I'm nearly nine-and-twenty. I think if I were to form a lasting passion I'd have done it before now. I'm quite willing to take a wife I like and respect—"

"Only?" she prompted.

"Only it seems as if I hardly need to marry Carolyn, as I can imagine what her reply would be to any possible topic of conversation."

"Oh, dear, I'm afraid that doesn't augur well for Carolyn."

"On the other hand, I'm not at all sure that an exciting marriage would suit me, either. I think I must be a very staid and conventional sort."

"You had responsibility thrust on you too young, my dear, but I don't think I would call you staid. When you find the *right* girl, you may be surprised at how unconventional you feel."

"Not all surprises are pleasant ones," he commented.

He turned his face to the fire, and covertly she studied him. His hair, darker now than the flaxen shade of his youth, gleamed a rich gold in the flickering light. His profile showed the high forehead, straight nose, rather determined chin, but gave no notion at all of the vulnerability of his mouth.

She did not think it was only a mother's prejudice; he was a handsome man, and any girl who was not attracted to his title, his fortune, or his manners would surely fall victim to his face—all too easily. Perhaps that was the trouble. She did not think him a vain man, but he could not fail to know that had he lifted his finger he could have had almost his choice of the accredited beauties on the Marriage Mart.

Had he ever really had a chance to enjoy a carefree season on the town? He was no sooner down from Oxford than his father had died, and the cares of the estate had descended upon him. When he went to London, he had an older sister already there and a younger one to follow. Perhaps he had been too distracted by family matters ever to indulge in the youthful follies of extravagant passions and writing sonnets to his beloved's dimple.

"Poor Robert," she said. "I'm afraid it's very dull here in the country at this time of year."

"Never in your presence, Mama. London is very dull this time of year, however, very thin of company. In fact, I thought to break my journey by visiting Eugenia for a few days on the way back."

"Oh, how fortuitous," she said brightly. "Then you can—" she broke off, "—unless of course you should dislike the idea too much."

"What idea, Mama?"

"Why, I'm sending Lily Griggs to Eugenia and—"

"Good heavens, don't tell me you're cutting down on the staff! Am I not allowing enough for household expenses?"

"Of course you are. I shall hire another maid to take her place. But poor Lily's young man didn't come up to scratch—after four years of keeping company. In fact, he has married Another. Now whenever she sees him in the village, she comes home and does nothing but weep. And Mrs. Baggers makes remarks. I think a change of scene is indicated . . . And Eugenia has also written to say that she will be pleased to engage the Broyles girl—Windom, I should say. I thought I would send them together. And if you took them in the carriage, it would serve beautifully. Lily hasn't a particle of sense, and while Miss Windom does, she hasn't any experience of travel at all. I don't suppose she has been ten miles from Gray Gables since Monty Broyles brought her home. Should you mind very much?" she asked anxiously.

"Mind?" he laughed. "It will be the highlight of the season. Only think—a trip in an enclosed carriage with a bluestocking governess and a lugubrious housemaid. You offer me a high treat, Mama!"

Chapter Three

As Cousin Frances had left to join her friend in Torquay the week before, and the late Monty Broyles's sister and daughters had returned to their own homes long since, Jessica's leavetaking was uncomplicated.

Only the housekeeper stood at the door as she left, and there was no warmth in her farewell. She was a tall, spare woman not above middle age, who had been employed in the household some ten years. Perhaps if she had been in residence when the orphaned child had been brought to Gray Gables hardly more than a babe, some maternal spark would have awakened in her breast, but when she arrived, Jessica was nearly eight years old, a self-sufficient little chit and clearly one who was not valued overmuch by the rest of the family, so no such sentiment was aroused.

The comfortable Markham traveling carriage had pulled up before the entrance of Gray Gables, and the viscount himself sprang down to escort Miss Windom down the steps. She had a subtly different air about her today, he thought. She was less the urchin, more the well-turned-out woman. No, that was not exactly the phrase. She still appeared absurdly young, and her clothes were not exactly the high kick of fashion—which would have been most inappropriate in a governess—but the dark blue pelisse, though modest, was well cut, and her bonnet, untrimmed save for a knot of grosgrain ribbon, framed her face becomingly.

Her portmanteau and a bandbox safely stowed away, she climbed into the carriage. She gave one brief look at Gray Gables and then settled back against the velvet squabs. "What a smashing carriage! Cousin Monty's was not a patch on it."

The viscount laughed. "I hope you're not planning to teach such slang to my nieces. Did you learn it from Harry?"

"I should imagine that as they have two brothers, there would be very little slang I could teach them." Then her face sobered. "And no, I have learned nothing from Harry. I picked that up from the stableboy—a very nice lad I used to bully into letting me take my cousin's horses out."

"I imagine you were quite a merciless bully," his lordship said, "being of such a great size and so fierce."

"And handy with my fives," she added wickedly.

They rode for some way in a silence which was broken only by muffled sobs coming from Lily Griggs's corner, as she was quite overcome at leaving the area where the "fondest hopes of her youth were trodden in the dust." Eventually she succeeded in crying herself to sleep, to the viscount's great relief.

"I hope that you were not too rushed making ready to remove to my sister's," Lord Markham said politely, at length.

"Not at all. I was glad to get away before Harry came home," she said so fervently that he raised startled eyes to her face.

Divining the direction of his thoughts, she said, "No, he never annoyed me, but he's the kind of odious little toad who was always kissing parlormaids in dark hallways. I took great care not to let him notice I was growing up."

"Would the boy's father not have protected you?" he asked.

"Not he. He thought Harry was the *ne plus ultra*. He was forever extolling his virtues, saying what a lucky girl it would be whom Harry took to wife. Almost as if he were recommending him to me as the highest ideal of a husband a girl could ever aspire to." She gave a little shudder. "As for me, I thought Harry's sole virtue was that he was so often from home."

As the carriage rounded each bend, she looked out the windows with such eagerness that Markham wished there were something more interesting for her to see than stubbled fields overlain with patches of dingy snow. "I'm sorry we travel at such a dull time," he said.

"New sights can never be dull," she said, "but I imagine it must be beautiful in the spring. I should think that meadow would be a fairy carpet of wildflowers in a few weeks."

"What part of the country do you come from originally?" he asked idly and was amazed at the stricken look his careless question had brought to her face.

It was gone in an instant and she said woodenly, "I have no idea. You see, my cousin would give me the present moment only, not the past. I had to be grateful to him for my daily bread, but he would not give me myself—not even my *name* until—" she broke off.

"What do you mean?"

"Why, until I learned to read I thought my name was Jessie. But I had a gold locket around my neck with the name 'Jessica' engraved on the back. I asked the old housekeeper about it once, the one who was there when I was brought to Gray Gables. She knew nothing except that her master had been from home for some weeks and arrived with me in the care of a serving woman, whom he immediately released and sent away. She said I had been wearing the locket under my clothes when I came. I always wore it under my dress, and I suppose Cousin Monty never saw it or knew I had it. At any rate he never told me it was my true name.

"The only thing he ever told me was that I was a relative, an orphan, and that he had taken on the responsibility of caring for me. When I was older, I asked him if it was my mother or my father who was his cousin. He was more than a little in his cups at the time, I think. He looked at me with an unpleasant smile and said, 'You don't have a father.' I didn't understand what he meant and I said, 'But everyone has a father.' He said, 'You've no right to his name, though. You're a base-born brat and nobody but me would give you a home. Don't you forget it.'

"I didn't understand, but it sounded a very ugly thing to be. I asked him what it meant and he said it meant I was greatly beholden to him and that I mustn't ever get above myself because I had no name

32

at all. Somehow that almost comforted me, because at least it meant that my name wasn't Broyles—which I had always supposed it to be. Then I asked him what my father's name had been and he growled out, 'Windom, for all the good it will do you to know.' I wrote it out on a piece of paper and showed it to him. He began to laugh in a queer, drunken way and said, 'Yes, that was it, but you'll never be able to claim it.' And so I have called myself Jessica Windom ever since, because though I have no right to it, my father is dead and surely would not grudge me the use of it."

There seemed a wistful plea in the last words, which, taken together with the sad little tale, stabbed at the viscount's pity so that he said very kindly, "No, indeed, I'm sure he would not. In fact he would be very proud, I should think, to have such an intelligent and accomplished young lady bear his name."

She gave him a sudden smile of pure gratitude that quite transformed her face.

"Look, we are coming to Elvaston," he said, hoping to distract her mind from past miseries. "If you look out on the right, you will see a very pretty little Norman church."

They broke their journey at Gurneymere, where they enjoyed a hearty tea. The inn had no private dining rooms available, but Jessica seemed quite entranced with the bustle and noise of the public room, and the viscount wondered if it were perhaps the first time she had ever eaten in an inn. They were seated near the fire, which was welcome as the air was raw and a bitter wind had risen.

During the afternoon, despite her apparent desire

not to miss any of the—to the viscount—indifferent sights of the journey, the swaying of the carriage had a lulling effect and sent Jessica into an hour's doze. At one point her head fell lightly against the viscount's shoulder. She was such a little thing that her weight was no burden. A bump in the road half-roused her and she repositioned herself in the corner.

When at last she awoke, she looked around with self-reproach. "Oh, I've been asleep. Have I missed anything?" she inquired.

Lord Markham laughed. "Wondrous sights. Two cathedrals, four snow-capped mountain peaks, and a mighty waterfall, not to mention the herd of unicorns that crossed the road in front of us."

She gave a reproving little giggle. "Very well, you are roasting me, but though you have passed this way countless times, I have not and am finding it all very interesting."

"Well, perhaps it was only a herd of cows and not unicorns at all," he admitted, "but I stand firm on the mountain peaks."

The afternoon wore on, and he had just observed that in not above two hours they would find themselves at the gates of Harewood Hall, when they felt a numbing jolt followed by a sickening lurch of the carriage, which tilted it to an uncomfortable angle. The viscount swore softly and thrust his head through the window to inquire of the coachman. After a brief colloquy he drew in again and asked the women if they found themselves undamaged.

They reassured him on that point, each having discovered herself to be only shaken about somewhat, whereupon he forced the door upward and clambered out. Not many minutes passed before his head reappeared in the doorway and he informed his fellow passengers that the wheel had struck a boulder in the road and was broken beyond repair.

"There's a small inn about a mile and a half down the road, where I make no doubt we can put up for the night," he said. "I will walk there and hire some sort of conveyance to transport you there. You will be quite safe with the coachman and postillions to guard you."

"But that is scarcely necessary," Jessica protested. "A mile and a half is no distance at all. I should as lief be walking as sitting still in this carriage."

"It is very cold out," he warned.

"I daresay we will be no colder walking than sitting still," she said stoutly, "and not nearly as uncomfortable as being cramped in this strange position. If we walk with you it will save time and trouble."

"Very well," he agreed. "Give me your hand and I will help you climb out."

For the first half-mile or so, despite the cold, it was a relief to be moving about after sitting for so many hours, but then a thin sleet began to fall. After about ten minutes of having the icy wetness flung in her face by the wind, Jessica began to wonder if it had been wise to leave the shelter of the carriage after all. Still it could not be so very much farther to the inn, and they would soon be warm again.

By the time the inn was in sight they were thoroughly chilled, and Jessica could feel her teeth chattering.

Lord Markham flung open the door and called for the landlord. In only a moment they were being led to the welcoming blaze of a roaring fire in a private parlor. "Here, take off your wet pelisse," he said, helping her. "I will go and arrange for rooms and some supper."

Both girls held out their hands to the blaze but neither could stop shivering. Before long the viscount returned to report that an adequate room was available for Miss Windom with a truckle bed for Lily, and that he had ordered a bowl of hot punch, which would soon warm them while they awaited their supper.

The landlord himself brought in the punch, and Lord Markham ladled it out for them. Jessica gulped at the aromatic beverage eagerly. It was hot and spicy and sweet with fruit juices and some other flavoring which she did not recognize. It was warming and delicious going down her throat, and she began to feel very much better indeed.

Lily, too, stopped shivering and accepted a second cup.

"Will Lady Harewood be very worried about you, do you think?" Jessica asked the viscount.

"I shouldn't think so. The weather must be as bad at Harewood Hall as it is here. She will doubtless think the icy rain has slowed us up so that we have had to go to ground for the night."

Jessica could feel a delightful warmth spreading all through her, banishing the recent chill, and she sat contentedly sipping her punch until suddenly she was startled by a cry from Lily. "My letters!"

"What?" Lord Markham demanded.

"He never gave me back my letters!" she exclaimed with a stricken look.

"What letters are you talking about?" Jessica asked.

"I can read and write," Lily asserted rather pugnaciously. "I write a good letter. I used to write to my intended—personal letters they was, for his eyes only."

"Love letters," Jessica deduced.

"He never returned them when he took up with that woman," Lily said darkly. "He'll let her read them—all my personal writings—and she'll laugh and probably tell them all over the village."

"Oh, I shouldn't think so," Jessica said sensibly. "He's doubtless burned them long since."

"Burn my letters? Not him. Likely saved them on purpose to show to her," she said bitterly and burst into tears.

As she wailed louder, the viscount, trying to hide his irritation, added his assurance that her intended had surely never displayed her letters to his new wife, but she refused to be comforted and sat dripping tears onto her lap and sobbing lustily.

Jessica shook her head ruefully and commented, "*Sed mulier cupido quod dicit amanti, In ventro scribere oportet aqua.*"

At that Lily broke off sobbing to demand, "What heathenish jibberish are you saying? It sounds like you're putting a curse on me and I never done nothing bad. I only wrote letters."

"No, no," Jessica soothed. "It's only something Catullus said. It just means, 'But a woman's sayings to her lover, Should be in wind and running water writ.'"

And then she saw Lord Markham's astonished eyes

upon her, she explained, "I only meant it as a simple jest, because while that was not precisely what Catullus meant, if Lily *had* confined her words to wind and running water instead of committing them to paper, she wouldn't be in this troubled frame of mind now."

But still he stared at her in such a way that she clapped a hand to her mouth in dismay and said, "My wretched tongue! I think something in that punch must have loosened it, because previously I had been so careful not to give offense by quoting anything or making foreign puns."

Though he was not unused to the rum which was in the punch, perhaps it had affected Lord Markham just a little, too, for he said in a highly affronted way, "Do you mean to tell me, my girl, that you have been patronizing me by refraining from showing your erudition lest you *offend* me?"

"Well, Chesterfield was probably right when he said, 'Wear your learning, like your watch, in a private pocket: and do not just pull it out and strike it; merely to show that you have one.'" And then creasing her brow in consternation, she said, "Oh, dear, I just did it again!"

Lord Markham pulled himself up stiffly. "I do not aspire to such erudition as Miss Windom's," he said with elaborate sarcasm, "but my years at Oxford were not *entirely* wasted. I give you my permission to quote as much as you like in English, Latin, Greek, or any other language in which you find yourself proficient. I do not think I shall find myself totally at a loss."

Stung by his tone, she replied, "I shan't avail myself of your permission because as Ovid said, '*Abeunt stu-*

dia in mores,' and I've made one enemy before today in such a way."

"More heathen talk," came a cry from Lily. "Was that about me?"

"No," Lord Markham said with a reprehensible gleam of triumph. "It merely means, 'Pursuits assiduously followed become habits,' and Miss Windom does not wish to cultivate the habit of talking down to her intellectual inferiors."

"Ah, the *coup de fond,*" Jessica murmured.

At that moment a serving girl brought in a great tray holding a leg of mutton surrounded by roast potatoes and vegetables, and the viscount with a wicked look exclaimed, *"Broma theon!"*

"Food for the gods, Lily. That's all it means," Jessica translated scornfully. "Perhaps eating will clear our heads." She turned to Lord Markham, inquiring, "You do intend for Lily to stay, as a sort of abigail, do you not?"

"Certainly," he said, "though why it should have crossed your mind that you need a chaperone I do not understand. I always believed *omnia munda mundis.*"

Taking exception to his tone, she smiled and said dulcetly, "Yes, indeed. To the pure all things are pure. However, I have always preferred that sentiment rendered in the original Greek: *pánta kathará toís katharoás.*"

And turning rather grandly to Lily, she said, "Come, let us take our places at the table."

Chapter Four

The next morning Jessica came downstairs to face Lord Markham with some trepidation. She had a strong sense of having behaved badly and to have been led to behave still more rudely by his scathing tongue. She had been unwise to risk making an enemy of the man whose sister would be her employer. She hardly knew how to meet his eyes.

There was some stiffness on both sides as they partook of coffee and rolls, but neither alluded to the previous evening's events.

Lily's eyes were still red and puffy, but her manner was less lugubrious and she actually seemed to look forward to reaching her new place of employment.

The broken carriage wheel took some little time to replace, the weather having been too inclement to have accomplished it the night before, so that it was nearly noon before the party was again on the road. By the time they had been an hour on the way, the sun unexpectedly broke through, transforming the layer of ice clinging to the trees and hedges into a glitter of diamond brilliance. Before they drove many miles it melted off, but Jessica had found it breathtaking while it lasted. Then the clouds covered the sun again and the prospect turned dismal once more.

Presently they found themselves passing beside a great forest, and the viscount said, "These woods belong to his Grace, the Duke of Salford. When we pass the crest of the hill ahead, we will be able to see my brother-in-law's land."

As the carriage turned into the long drive of Harewood Hall, she peered eagerly out the window to catch her first glimpse of her new home. It was a handsome Palladian house of perhaps some hundred and fifty years, built of a cream stone. The front was perfectly symmetrical, with the railings at the sides of the entrance steps curving outward in pleasing arcs. The house was topped by a hipped roof from which a series of dormer windows projected, and in the center was set an imposing octagonal cupola.

As the carriage rolled to a stop, a footman appeared to assist the passengers in alighting. At the door stood a sober-faced butler to usher them in. She saw that the entrance was no mere vestibule but an impressive hall from which a graceful staircase, its balusters heavily carved, rose to a landing and branched outward to either side.

She had had time to do no more than look around when a tall woman with sparkling eyes, her blond hair coiled at the back of her slender neck, came running across the hall and threw herself at the viscount. "Robert, you wretch," she cried, kissing him soundly. "You had me worried to death. I imagined you overturned in a ditch or set upon by brigands."

"Such an excess of sensibility," Lord Markham reproved, "and when I had convinced Miss Windom that you would be reasonable enough to guess that we had merely taken snug refuge from the bad weather."

"Was *that* all?" she asked.

"Well, actually a broken wheel influenced our decision," he admitted with a twinkle as he turned to make her acquainted with Jessica.

"Miss Windom, what an uncomfortable experience," she said, taking Jessica's hand warmly. "I hope you suffered no ill effects." She turned to Lily Griggs. "I'm so happy you will be with us, Lily. Here is our housekeeper, Mrs. Tallboys, who will show you around and take you under her wing.

"Come into the library for a moment and warm yourselves by the fire," she directed the others.

Jessica was immediately enchanted with the room. It was some fifty feet long, the far narrow wall composed almost entirely of swag-draped windows from which she caught a glimpse of the park beyond. The long walls were lined with bookshelves to the ceiling, save for a handsome fireplace surmounted by a large portrait on the left side and two windows on the right-hand wall with cozy seats built into them. The furniture consisted of a commodious writing desk, a six-sided marquetry table, a reading stand, a small tilt-top table, and several ingenious-looking sets of library steps. The chairs and sofas were mostly upholstered in tapestry of a soft rosy-red with a pattern of French blue leaves.

A footman who been unloading the luggage appeared in the doorway, and Lady Harewood said, "Lord Markham will have his usual room, Eppers. You didn't bring your man with you, Robert?"

"No, he most injudiciously contracted an infectious cold three days ago, and I sent him directly to London to recuperate in solitude. He loses all skill at starching my neckcloths whenever he suffers from some trifling complaint, anyway."

"Such a harsh employer," his sister murmured, giving his arm a squeeze. "Miss Windom, my daughters have so much been looking forward to your arrival. Here is Rose," she beckoned to a very young housemaid, "who will show you to your room. I'm sure you will want to tidy up, and when you come down, we will have tea here in the library and you can meet the girls."

Jessica followed Rose up the graceful staircase, then down a corridor to a smaller staircase which led to the top story. "The nursery is just there, miss, and beyond it the schoolroom. And here is your bedchamber."

She opened the door and Jessica gasped with pleasure. The room was small but comfortably proportioned, with dormer windows and a neat fireplace. It was decorated all in yellow and white, with a dainty sprigged paper on the walls, white curtains tied back with yellow cords, and a yellow striped reading chair placed near the window. The tent bed had a yellow spread and hangings. On a small writing table stood a jug in which were three white roses and a variety of greenery.

"Oh, what a charming room," she exclaimed. "Even on a dark day such as this it seems cheerful."

"The greenhouse is rather bare just now, but the gardener let me have those roses and greens to welcome you," the little maid said.

"What a thoughtful thing to do, and how prettily you have arranged them. You must have a great knack."

Rose flushed with pleasure. "Shall I unpack for you, miss?"

"I can do that," Jessica said, opening her portmanteau. "I must change out of this travel dress. I'm afraid I stained it badly walking in the wet last night, and tore my petticoat as well."

"Just give them to me, miss. I'll see to having your dress made clean and stitch up your petticoat too."

"I'd be most grateful if my dress could be cleaned, but don't worry yourself over the petticoat. I've done all the mending at my home for—oh, for years and years."

"Would you like the fire lit? Madame said you were to have one whenever you wished."

"How kind of her! But no, I don't need one now. I shall be going down presently to meet my new charges." She slipped out of her dress and handed it to Rose. "There you are. I'll see to the unpacking. And thank you so much for the pretty posy. It makes me feel very welcome indeed."

As the door closed behind the little maid, Jessica thought gratefully that she had found one friend in this new home. She only hoped that she would find two more in her pupils.

After washing her face and hands and tidying her hair, she put on a neat dress of gray twill and squared her shoulders to go downstairs. The house was such a large one that she hoped she wouldn't become lost.

She was just approaching the staircase when a door opened and out popped a boy of about thirteen. He had straw-colored hair but his brows, above bright blue eyes, were dark and arched upward rather dramatically. The satanic brows in such a young and innocent face seemed so incongruous that she felt instantly intrigued by the child.

"You're the new governess, aren't you? I'm Claire and Delphie's brother Phillip."

"Yes, I'm Miss Windom. I'm very happy to know you, Phillip."

"I expect I'll see you again, often, unless Claire drives you away," he said and popped back into his room.

She started to descend the stairs and had rounded the curve to the landing when, to her astonishment, she saw Phillip standing there below her. "Goodness, you startled me," she told him. "How did you get here ahead of me?" The staircase above the landing branched off in the other direction, but she did not see any way he could have gotten from the room into which she had seen him disappear over to the other side so quickly.

"I move very fast," he said. "I told you you'd see me often. Would you like to see my frogs?"

"Another time I'd like to very much, but your mama is waiting for me now."

"You do *like* frogs, don't you?" he asked, not moving out of her way.

"I'm very partial to them," she said solemnly, "but I really must go now." He stood aside and let her pass. She had just reached the bottom of the staircase when she looked ahead to see him waiting for her in the hall. Really shaken now, she whirled to look upward at the empty landing, then back at Phillip. "How did you manage to do that?" she demanded.

"Do what?" he asked innocently.

"Get down here from the landing."

"Haven't you ever known anyone who could be in two places at the same time?"

"No, I haven't," she said, rather unsteadily.

"Well, now you do," he told her and strolled off.

She stared after him, wondering if her senses were disordered. By the time she reached the door of the library, she was thoroughly discomposed and answered several of Lady Harewood's questions quite at random.

The viscount was there, lounging against the fireplace and regarding her with a curious eye. His sister, who put down Jessica's distraction to shyness in a new situation, kindly said, "I'll ring for tea now and have the girls come down if you feel up to meeting them so soon after your journey. But we shan't inflict the twins on you until after you are thoroughly rested."

"Twins?" Jessica's head snapped up.

"My sons, Peter and Phillip, who are a year younger than Claire."

"Are they—are they very much alike, ma'am?" Jessica inquired.

"Like peas in a pod."

"Then I fancy I have met them already," she said in a tone of heartfelt relief.

"Oh, ho," came from Lord Markham. "I begin to suspect those young scoundrels have been up to mischief."

"Not at all," Jessica disclaimed. "One of them—Peter, I believe—even offered to show me his frogs."

When the girls were summoned, they arrived so promptly that it was obvious they had been hovering nearby, consumed with curiosity about their new governess.

Claire at fourteen gave promise of being tall like her mother, but her recent illness had left a look of fragility about her. Her sweet, heart-shaped face was very pale and she was far too thin.

Five-year-old Delphina, on the other hand, was distinctly overweight, rather roly-poly in shape, but she too had a pale complexion. Perhaps, Jessica thought, since her sister's illness Delphie had been somewhat overlooked and had not been getting enough exercise. She seemed a taking little thing, however. Standing gravely before Jessica, she confided, "I've never had a governess before."

"Well, I'll tell you a secret," Jessica said. "I've never had a pupil before either, so we shall have to help each other go on properly, shall we not?"

She noted as the girls helped themselves from the sumptuous tea tray that Claire scarcely took anything, while Delphie heaped her plate with cakes and sweetmeats.

She encouraged the older girl to talk about her

school in Chelsea and her studies, and she learned that Claire had been fairly proficient on the pianoforte before her illness, but had not practiced since then. "Miss Windom is prepared to teach you to play the harp and will doubtless be vastly disappointed if you don't allow her to make full use of her expertise," the viscount said.

Jessica gave him a quelling look. "I think one instrument is quite enough at a time, especially since Claire has not fully regained her health," she said, thereby gaining a look of gratitude from the rather alarmed Claire. "Actually the harp requires a certain amount of strength to play properly, despite its look of delicacy."

Teatime passed off without any further awkwardness, and Jessica learned that she was expected to dine with the family that evening. Though the girls' lessons would not begin until the morrow, Jessica asked if they would show her the schoolroom and offered to read to them for a while.

She was in some doubt as to which dress would be most appropriate to wear to dinner. Lady Sarah's parting gift to her, over her own protests, had been a length of heavy green silk which had been made into a modest but well-cut evening dress. It was perfectly correct for a governess, yet it had a look of quiet elegance. She had objected that she would have no need for such a gown, but Lady Sarah had been firm. "The occasion might arise," she had said, "and it will give you a feeling of confidence to know that you are prepared."

Briefly she considered it now, as she could have used something to give her confidence facing her first dinner in a great house, but she rejected the idea lest she appear overdressed and chose instead the wine-colored kerseymere made from the cloth that Cousin Frances had given her. It had a lace fichu, and she thought it should serve nicely.

Meeting Lord Harewood proved to be no ordeal, as he seemed a kind if rather offhand gentleman. Two neighbors added to the party, so they were six at table.

Covertly Lord Markham watched Jessica and thought that Lady Sarah must be held accountable for her exquisite manners. Certainly she had not learned to conduct herself with such easy grace at Gray Gables. He knew that she had never dined in such surroundings or been offered such a bewildering array of dishes, and yet she never made a false move and all the while conversed pleasantly with Sir Thomas Forstman. Only once he saw her eyes light with sudden fire as if Sir Thomas had said something with which she violently disagreed, but instantly she checked the words he sensed were trembling on her tongue and returned instead a noncommittal answer.

Since he felt that he himself was in part responsible for her being at Harewood Hall, he was glad that he would be able to give his mother a good account of her. For a moment there in the inn last night, he had had the most uncomfortable suspicion that she was too independent, too much of an original, ever to fit into the docile mold of governess. He was relieved to find himself wrong on that score.

* * *

On the morning he was to leave, as his luggage was being stowed in the carriage, he was just crossing the great hall when Jessica came out of the library. He was already wearing his many-caped traveling coat, and despite his valet's defection his top boots gleamed. He stood looking down at her. "Well, Miss Windom, so your new career has begun."

"Yes, and I thank you, sir, for the suggestion that I might fill the position, as well as for conveying me here in such comfort."

"Yes, a broken wheel and a walk through an ice storm are no doubt your idea of perfect comfort," he said with a mocking smile.

"Those were merely trifles, and I'm sure your carriage was a hundred times nicer than the common stage would have been."

"I wish you success in your venture," he said lightly, and could not resist adding, "By the time I next see my nieces, I shall expect to find them turned into pattern cards of perfection and propriety, just like their teacher."

She flushed, remembering with how little propriety she had behaved, wrangling with him in that rude way at the inn, but she bit back the indignant retort that had trembled at her lips and merely wished him a cool farewell.

Chapter Five

Setting up a schedule for Delphie's lessons proved not difficult at all, as the child seemed more than ready to start her schooling and apparently thrived on the attention her new governess accorded her.

Jessica did not have such an easy time with Claire. Each new subject she broached, Claire objected to on the grounds that she had already mastered it at her school, or alternatively that it was too advanced. Eventually Jessica came to the conclusion that for the past months Claire had been enjoying her vacation from books and had no wish to tax her mind now with a serious rededication to study.

She decided to try out a period of review that would not be difficult enough to turn Claire rebellious and would at the same time help Jessica assess the extent of her knowledge.

Delphie's nanny, Maude Weems, who had been at Ashendene when Lady Harewood was a child, seemed to be a permanent fixture of the household and was accustomed to presiding over the nursery teas. It was from her that Jessica met her first real opposition. She discovered that Delphie ate far too many sweets and little else, and that cakes and pastries were provided in abundance. She took it upon herself to speak to Cook and suggest that henceforth the nursery trays were to hold meat, cheese, or a boiled egg, bread and butter, fresh fruit, and never more than one simple sweet.

Maud Weems at once took umbrage and reported to Lady Harewood that the new governess was a bit above herself and trying to starve poor Claire and Delphie in the bargain. Nanny had been too many years in the household to be ignored, so Lady Harewood paid a visit to the nursery at teatime. It seemed to her that the repast was ample to feed the girls, and she commented gaily, "What a nice meal you're having."

Whereupon Delphie complained that plain custard did not seem so very nice to her and why were there never any of her favorite sticky buns or currant cakes anymore?

At this point Claire interposed that Delphie was a greedy little thing who stuffed herself too much and it was no wonder she was fat as a pig.

This observation brought a severe reprimand from her mother, but it also caused Lady Harewood to take a long look at her younger daughter and to wonder if what she had been accustomed to think of as mere baby fat had not now indeed gone beyond the line of what was pleasing.

In the end Miss Windom's instructions to Cook were upheld, but Jessica knew she had made an enemy of Nanny.

The twins were not much in evidence, as they

shared their lessons with the younger Forstman boys. The tutor, Mr. Murdock, had previously resided at Harewood Hall, but at the time of Claire's illness, in order to provide a quieter household, he had removed to the Forstman place, where the twins now went daily for their lessons.

Since Miss Windom had not complained to their mother of their mischievous behavior on her first day, they were disposed to think well of her, especially when later she handled their frog collection with every evidence of interest and none at all of squeamishness. And on one occasion when the twins, facing a Latin competition which Mr. Murdock had designed between them and the Forstman boys, had slipped off to attend a fair instead of studying, Miss Windom drilled them privately at the last moment by such an effective method that they came off quite creditably in the competition and afterward pronounced her a regular right 'un.

The chilly weather gave way to the gentle hand of spring, and it would not be long before they would be able to spend some time outdoors. Jessica had determined that some lessons in the fresh air would have a beneficial effect on both her pupils. Delphie was by degrees beginning to lose some of her pudgy look, though her complexion was still more pasty than Jessica could approve. Claire was growing stronger, though she had as great a reluctance as before really to apply herself to her books. One day in exasperation Jessica pointed out to her that she assuredly had the ability to learn but through her own laziness was wasting opportunities of becoming a well-educated young lady.

"But I don't *want* to become schooled and accomplished," Claire said with a stubborn little toss of her head.

Jessica's brows rose in amazement.

Claire clapped her hands dramatically to her ears. "Don't bother to tell me. I know exactly what you're going to say."

Interest kindled in Jessica's eyes. "Do you really? That's quite amazing!" she said admiringly. "I've never known anyone gifted with second sight before. Though once when I was about eight I met a gypsy woman coming through the woods who claimed to have it. She offered to tell my fortune if I would run home and bring her the silver sixpence I had hidden in my room. But she was quite out there because I didn't have a sixpence, so I can't think the fortune would have proved very accurate either. Perhaps you will tell my fortune for me one day."

"Don't be so nonsensical!" Claire cried, torn between ill humor and laughter. "You know that's not what I meant. I only meant that in this particular instance everyone always says the same thing, so of course you will too."

"Dear me, what a repetitive group of people you have been associating with," Jessica murmured. "And what *is* this thing that I am bound to say?"

"Why, that if I don't become an accomplished young lady I will never get a husband."

Jessica looked affronted. "I must say I never expected you to accuse me of telling a *plumper* like that!"

Claire looked quite thunderstruck. "Do you mean to say you consider it a fib that one must be accomplished in order to get a husband?"

"My dear child," Jessica said kindly, "there are various reasons why a man chooses a wife, but I have never heard it even hinted that a girl's proficiency at playing the pianoforte or use of the globes entered into the matter. If a girl is very rich and very pretty and excessively sweet-natured, she should have no difficulty at all in acquiring a husband. Sometimes just one of those qualities will suffice, especially if it is the first in the list."

Claire was staring at her governess in astonishment. "Then *why* should I stuff my head full of all sorts of useless information?" she managed to say.

"Well, there is always the possibility that when the time comes you won't want just any husband, but one special one. And if he should be quite intelligent, it would be agreeable if you could manage not to bore him. However, if that were the only consideration I shouldn't worry, because after all there are so many dull men around and you might equally well choose to marry one of those. No," she said thoughtfully, "the only real reason for learning is for your own sake. It may have escaped your notice, but this is a very interesting world we live in, and many interesting people have recorded their thoughts about it in one way and another in poetry, in painting, in politics, in classifying the plants, in calculating the wandering of the planets among the stars. Yes, Claire," she made an all-encompassing gesture, "there is an unimaginable wealth of fascinating knowledge in the world, and I can't think of any sadder way to cheat yourself than to fail to enrich your mind with as much of it as you can acquire."

Claire sat quietly with her eyes downcast.

"Picture a girl in a roomful of good foods," Jessica went on, "refusing to eat anything but cream cakes. She would soon grow fat and slow; her skin would lose its blush, her eyes their luster. And it would be so unnecessary, because all she would have to do is to choose to eat a variety of the wholesome foods available and she would have a healthy glow and a zest for life. Minds can be fed too many cream cakes, too, and then they become fat and lazy. When you do marry, how sad if you find yourself fit for nothing more interesting than counting the household linens. How terribly sad not to be able to enjoy good reading or discussing what the government is doing. How sad to walk through a field without understanding what you're seeing. How sad not to be able to appreciate the Lord's bounty and the genius of man. And real appreciation must be based on understanding."

Seeing that Claire had grown very quiet and thoughtful, she rose and said, "I think we will not have any more lessons today. Perhaps you would like to rest awhile. I shall go to my room and read."

The next day she was already drilling Delphie in her numbers when Claire entered the schoolroom. She handed Jessica an essay she had been assigned previously on the Wars of the Roses and sat down without a word, but from that time on Jessica vowed to herself that she would do everything in her power to make learning exciting and fun for both girls.

Lord Robert Markham returned to London, and while he was much too well mannered to be said to have dropped Carolyn Warriner, by degrees he subtly distanced himself from her. There were those who claimed that his interest had been caught by Lady Pamela Hasebrook.

There was no reason to complain that London was thin of company as the spring wore on and the Season began in earnest. Still the viscount willingly refused a number of invitations and left town when his bailiff at Ashendene wrote of urgent business at home.

His mother was delighted to see him as always, and tactfully refrained from questioning him about Carolyn Warriner.

"Oh, by the by," she told him one evening, "Harry Broyles finally turned up at Gray Gables. The vicar said he behaved most peculiarly. Seemed put out that his father had died without notice. And he was quite annoyed that Jessica had left. He even came to see me about it, questioning me about Harewood Hall. The man has no more manners than a pump handle. When I explained her situation in some detail, he finally said, 'Oh, well, I suppose she'll be safe enough there for the present.' I said, 'Safe enough? In my daughter's home? Indeed I should think so, and a good deal better off than at Gray Gables with no one to chaperone her.' He's been up to London several times since then, but no one seems to know what his plans are for the property or if indeed he has any."

"Perhaps I shall see Miss Windom soon, as I plan to spend a night with Eugenia on my way back to London," the viscount said.

"Splendid, my dear. She will be very glad to see you. And you can take to her some of Cook's latest batch of ginger marmalade, for I'm sure I shall never be able to use half of it. If you should not object, of course."

"You are losing your touch, Mama," he said, his lips quivering. "Such a tame commission after the last one you entrusted to me. I daresay a shipment of ginger marmalade will not be half so fatiguing as Lucy Griggs and Miss Windom. Nor so diverting either."

On his arrival at Harewood Hall, the viscount thought from the sight of his nieces that Miss Windom had been doing her job creditably. Delphie had slimmed down and was not so inclined to chatter aimlessly. Claire, though she was still thin, had lost her look of die-away boredom.

He could not, of course, visit the house without seeing his old nanny. As usual, she warned him that it was obvious he had been keeping too late hours, that dissipation would cause him to lose his looks, and that it was past time for him to set up his nursery.

He only laughed, for Nanny always exercised her prerogative of scolding anyone whom she had cared for as an infant, and it was impossible for him to take umbrage at her animadversions.

"My nieces are looking well, I think," he said to change the subject. "I think Miss Windom's efforts must be proving satisfactory. Delphie is become quite the civilized young lady."

Nanny sniffed ominously. "That's as may be," she said.

"Come, Nanny, don't ruffle your feathers at me. You know the girls are in good hands. Claire even asked me several intelligent questions about the new collection at the British Museum."

"Good hands you may call them, but my babes won't be in those hands much longer. Your Miss Know-all's job is nearly finished here."

"What on earth can you mean?" he chided. "It has barely begun. Why, Delphie's only five."

"Humph! There may be them as thinks that educating those babes was the one job that governess came here to do, but Maude Weems isn't such an innocent."

"Explain yourself," he said sharply, beginning to feel irritated. "What other job can you imagine she came here to do?"

"Why, to get herself a husband, the same as any other flighty young chit."

He laughed. "I think flighty is a very poor description of the ever-practical Miss Windom," he said. "And as for husbands—why, my nephews are a trifle young to catch her fancy, do you not think?"

"Even a top-lofty one like her could hardly look to Quality for a husband, poor as she is and no family worth mentioning. But there's other easy enough pickings for one with her wiles. She's turned the curate up sweet as honey, and you mark my words, the banns will be read before the month is out."

"Mr. *Rountree*?" the viscount said in astonishment.

"The same," she pronounced portentously. "And for all that his income isn't above seventy pounds a year, to an orphan girl with no prospects, that would look like a step up in the world."

He took his leave of her rather abruptly.

Later in the day, returning from the stables, he met with Miss Windom, who was returning to the house with some schoolbooks after a lesson in the garden.

She greeted him in a friendly way and inquired after the health of his mother. After he had answered, they walked together in silence, he feeling quite out of charity with her. He was conscious of a sense of ill usage. After he had proposed her for a position in his sister's house and conveyed her here in his own carriage, it seemed to him the least she could have done was stay on above a few months instead of running off with the curate, whom he realized now he had always considered a particularly boring and pretentious man.

"Do you find your nieces well?" she asked at length.

"Very well," he said rather shortly. "They seem devoted to you. It is only a pity that you will not be with them much longer, as your influence has surely been most salutary."

She stiffened. "I was not aware that I had failed to give satisfaction. Lady Harewood is so kindly disposed that she doubtless found it difficult to tell me that I was to be dismissed."

"No, no. You misunderstand me. I'm sure my sister

is most pleased. What I meant was that I had been led to believe you were contemplating matrimony."

She stared blankly at him.

Even as he spoke, he was aware of the impropriety of broaching such a subject, but he could not seem to check the words. "You have made quite a conquest of the curate, I believe."

"Mr. *Rountree*?" she exclaimed in astonishment. "Matrimony with a man of so little consequence? Scarcely!"

Though her disclaimer was in no way unwelcome, his embarrassment at his own bad manners led him to say contentiously, "You would only consider marriage to a man of consequence, then?"

A fine flush crept over her face, but it was a flush of anger. "Very true, my lord, but I think the word has a different connotation for you than for me. To you a man of consequence is one of rank and fortune. To me he is one of intelligence and character."

"You judge poor Mr. Rountree harshly," he said.

"Perhaps, but not unjustly. And as for matrimony, Mr. Rountree's infatuation dates from his seeing a letter to me written by Lady Sarah while she was visiting her father and bearing his frank. Upon learning from Lady Harewood that I stood high in the affection of an earl's daughter and was on close terms with her, his interest in me began to blossom. He has not been so impertinent as to mention marriage, but I assure you that should he do so, it will avail him nothing. I am very well satisfied with my position here, and even if your sister had proved a harsh mistress and your nieces demons, I should still prefer it to being leg-shackled to an encroaching popinjay like Mr. Rountree."

With that she whirled abruptly on her heel and left Lord Markham standing somewhat agape in the drive. He did not encounter her again before he left for London.

Chapter Six

Lord Harewood had generously offered Jessica a choice of mounts from his stable, and she took the keenest delight in riding though she had little time away from her charges to indulge herself in the pastime. Delphie was too young to ride more than a gentle pony, and the doctor deemed it too strenuous an exercise for Claire to undertake as yet.

One afternoon Lady Harewood joined the nursery party at teatime just as Jessica had been describing a charming copse the other side of the north pasture and asking if they were familiar with it.

"Oh, Mama," Claire cried, "do you remember the spot where we used to go to pick bluebells? Miss Windom says it is a carpet of wildflowers now. Could we not go and have our lessons there on fine days? Dr. Dartney says the fresh air is good for me, and I'm tired of going only as far as the garden."

"We could take a lunch basket!" cried Delphie, clapping her hands, for though she had with fairly good grace given up consuming such large quantities of sweets as she had formerly enjoyed, she had by no means lost her interest in food.

"Well," her mother said, "perhaps Miss Windom could ride and you two could go in the pony cart. I do not think Claire should try to drive, but perhaps Jemmy Dawson could be spared to go with you."

"Jemmy is our undergroom's son," Claire explained to Jessica. "Oh, Mama, I do think it is prime of you to let us do it."

"*Not* one of the phrases I have been at pains to teach her, ma'am," Jessica said, her eyes twinkling.

"I never thought it," her employer replied, "but we shouldn't have to look far to find the imps who did."

The outings proved highly satisfactory to all parties involved. The change of scene lent new enchantment to lessons. Jessica enjoyed her ride, cantering beyond the copse and then returning to meet the arrival of the pony cart, which had traveled at a more sedate pace. Jemmy looked after the horse and pony, shared their lunch basket, and since Delphie's span of attention to lessons was much shorter than Claire's and Jessica allowed her to spend part of her time running and playing, his duties included watching to see that she did not wander too far afield or fall into the stream.

Both girls started wildflower collections, and because Delphie had so much more time to search them out, hers held the greater number of specimens, to her great pride.

One day when Jessica went to fetch Delphie to make ready to start home, she found her standing scornfully, hands on hips, berating Jemmy Dawson. "That's just babyish the way you've made your *es*.

They're all backward. *E*s are *very* easy because they point to the east."

Jessica saw she was examining some scratching in the dirt made with a stick. When Jemmy saw the governess observing them, he dropped his stick, turned fiery red, and twisted his cap further over his eyes.

Jessica handed Delphie a flower she was carrying and said, "Take this back to Claire and see if she can find it in the wildflower book, will you please, Delphie? And then start packing up."

When the little girl had scampered off, Jessica examined the scratching in the dirt more closely and found it, though with the *e*s indeed reversed, to read, "Reading is to the mind what exercise is to the body."

"You have a good memory, Jemmy," she commented.

He cast her a scared look. "Sometimes when I've finished with the horses and just sitting waiting, I can't help overhearing the lessons, miss."

"Why shouldn't you listen, Jemmy? Do you like lessons?"

"Like 'em, miss? I dunno. Never heard any before. Numbers is easier than letters, ain't they? But some of the stories you tell is capital. That one about Hannibal was *prime*!"

She smiled. "Tomorrow I'll bring you a slate and you can join our circle while we have lessons."

He squinted doubtfully at her. "The master wouldn't cut up over it, would he? Me dad would skin me if he did."

"I can't think of a reason why he would object. You

might as well share our lessons as sit there bored and wasting time." She infused her tone with more confidence than she felt, but if Lord Harewood should find out and object, she would take the responsibility, for the challenge of a hungry mind was one she couldn't turn her back on.

On the next two days a chill wind kept the schoolroom party indoors, but it was followed by a week of hot and sunny weather. It seemed to Jessica that each day the rosy color in the girls' cheeks glowed more healthily.

They accepted Jemmy's participation in their lessons with good nature which was perhaps a little patronizing, until by the end of the week it occurred to Claire that he was quicker at number problems than she was.

That day when Jessica returned her horse to the stable, the girls had already unloaded the pony cart and gone up to the house. Jemmy came to help her dismount. "You're doing very well with your lessons, Jemmy," she told him.

He scuffed his toe in the dirt but looked pleased at the praise.

"Have you ever thought about what you want to be when you grow up?"

He looked up, surprised. "Why, a groom, miss. What else?"

"Do you like horses a great deal?"

He scratched his head. "Like them? Well, nothing to boast of. But me dad is a groom and me granddad afore him."

"Is there something you'd like better?" she persisted.

He seemed puzzled. "Well, miss, the only jobs I know much about is horses and farming, and of the two I think I'd like farming best. But I've got to be a groom a'cos that's what I'm trained for."

"Suppose you could have any job you liked. What would you choose?"

He considered. "Well, I guess I'd like Mr. Grammidge's job."

"The bailiff? Why?"

"A'cos he collects the rents," he said simply.

Jessica laughed and handed over the reins to him.

The fine summer wore on. Claire's health was so much improved that there was talk of sending her back to school, but Lady Harewood had had such a fright the previous year when she had become so ill that she scarcely wished to let her daughter leave home again, and Lord Harewood concurred that Claire seemed to be learning more from Miss Windom than she had at school.

Jessica was pleased with their decision, because though Lady Harewood had assured her they wanted her to stay on to teach Delphie in any case, having two pupils, especially one of Claire's age, provided more of a challenge.

Late in the summer Lord Markham paid a surprise visit to his sister and her husband, arriving late in the evening on his way down from London. His sister was always delighted to see him, but he could only promise to stay two nights as he had pressing business at Ashendene.

Next day his brother-in-law had risen before him and gone out, so the viscount ate a solitary breakfast and was just leaving the house for a morning ride when he was intercepted by Nanny. After their last encounter he was a little irritated at seeing her, for he felt that the false story she had told him had caused him to behave with unwonted bad manners toward Miss Windom.

"Weren't you coming to see me today, Master Robert?" she inquired in an aggrieved tone.

"I didn't know you rose so early," he said lightly.

"Humph," she sniffed. "*I'm* not one to shirk my duties, though there's some in this house that couldn't say the same."

"Now, Nanny, I don't want to hear tale-bearing. This isn't my house and I'm not responsible for its staff."

"Responsible for one of them, you are. Brought her here, you did."

"Come now," he said coolly. "I don't know why you've taken Miss Windom in aversion, nor do I care, but I don't want to hear any more tittle-tattle."

"You'll notice she never managed to bring it off with the curate after all," she said triumphantly as if scoring a point, for all the world as if it had not been *she* who had predicted the match in the first place. "Caught on to her sly ways, he did."

"I'm sorry, Nanny, but I must bid you good morning. I'm going for a ride now," he said firmly and started down the passage.

"A ride, is it? Then if you keep your eyes open, like as not you'll see for yourself. Spends a powerful lot of time in the stables, that governess does. Teaching the horses to talk, I *don't* think! I don't know who she meets on the sly down there, but you can bank on it that Mr. Rountree found out what she is and that's why he wouldn't have her."

"You are not to spread tales like that," he said, rounding on her sharply. "Miss Windom has a right to ride whenever she pleases, for my brother-in-law has told me so."

"I've lived enough years to know whether a female is dressed in riding clothes or not," she said maliciously. "And she wasn't when she sneaked out this morning to meet whoever it is she meets down there. You'll see," she called after him.

Lord Markham was experiencing fury as he crossed the courtyard. Damn all gossiping women anyway. If Miss Windom was at the stables it was doubtless on a perfectly harmless errand, but to go there now made it look as if he were spying on her. However, he had announced his intention to ride; he was dressed for riding; if he didn't go it would seem as if he were afraid of what he would find. Which was ridiculous. It was nothing to him one way or another, personally, though he would be disturbed if a girl he and his mother had introduced into this household should behave shabbily. But she wouldn't. He was confident of that.

As he approached the stables, he called out, but no one appeared, so he entered. The place seemed deserted. He walked to the stall where Chevron was waiting, patted the velvet nose, and produced a lump of sugar. He was on the point of opening the door to lead him out when he heard a voice nearby—Miss Windom's voice, warm and low. "Oh, you're remarkable; you really are. You can't imagine how happy you make me."

A feeling of sickness flooded over the viscount. He did not stop to assess his reaction of disgust and betrayal. He took a hasty step backward, startling one of the other horses, who whickered.

At that the tack-room door opened and a small figure slipped out. "Excuse me, miss, someone must have come into the stable. Oh, it's you, sir. Was you wanting Chevron saddled?"

"If you please," the viscount answered automatically.

The door opened further and he saw Miss Windom framed in the doorway. "Oh, Lord Markham, I'm glad to see you. Would you come in here a moment, please?"

Bewildered, he followed her. "I've been wishing for an opportunity to ask your advice. Look at this, will you?" She handed him a sheet of paper. He could hardly concentrate on it, but it seemed to be covered with figures.

"Not one answer wrong!" she said exultantly. "Can you believe Jemmy never had any schooling at all until this summer?"

"I'm afraid I don't understand," he said.

"Jemmy Dawson; the little groom. He drove the girls in the pony cart when we had lessons down in the copse. He never seemed to be paying attention to the lessons, but his mind was just so starved for learning that he stored everything up. I found out quite by accident and asked him to join us. Of course in bad weather we couldn't go out, so I've been giving him extra lessons here in the tack room, and his progress surpasses anything you could credit. He has a special affinity for mathematics and already is advanced of Claire, though of course she is not very interested in the subject. But something must be done for him. He is far too bright at his books to have to go through life as a groom, which he doesn't have any real inclination for."

He had experienced such an odd sensation at the beginning of her story—was it relief?—that it was difficult for him to follow her discourse and understand what it was she wanted of him.

"Perhaps a charity school—" he began.

"No, no, that wouldn't do at all. I've looked into the matter and it's not in the least what Jemmy needs."

"Are you condemning charity schools out of hand?" he asked, a little affronted. "I believe they serve a useful function. I subscribe to one myself."

"Oh, yes, they are all very well and no doubt do a certain amount of good, but it wouldn't be right for Jemmy. You see, the whole basis of the charity school is to teach moral precepts, religious principles, virtues of thrift, and if possible a bit of reading and arithmetic—but not to the extent of making the children discontent with their station in life."

"And you find this objectionable?" he asked with brows raised.

She hesitated. "Well, that is not the point at the moment," she temporized, "though it would be no very bad thing if someday 'one's station in life' was nothing more than an outmoded idea. But right now my concern is with Jemmy, and he should *not* go to a school which teaches him to be satisfied with his station because what he must do is break out of the mold into which he has been cast. You don't realize it because you haven't worked with him as I have, but he is an exceptionally bright child—not just shrewd or quick-witted, but one with a real aptitude for books."

"I presume you're not proposing that I enter him for Harrow!"

She made a little moue of impatience. "You seem to think I'm quite woolly-minded, Lord Markham. And I *do* realize Jemmy isn't your problem. But I don't know anyone else who lives in London. I thought perhaps you could look into schools for me. There must be good places where the middle classes send their sons. Who knows what he could rise to—banking, engineering, farm management at the least. There must be some school like that with a charity subscription for students who can't pay."

"Well," he looked doubtful, "I can inquire, but would he fit in?"

"Not at the moment; not the way he talks and so on. I haven't dared to tamper with his speech yet, because until it's certain that something can be done for him, it won't do to set him apart from his peers. But it would be nothing short of criminal if something *can't* be done for him."

Before either of them could say more, Jemmy appeared in the door. "Chevron is getting a mite resty, my lord."

"Thank you." He turned to Jessica. "I'll see what I

can find out for you when I get back to London," he told her.

When he returned from his ride, he sought out his sister and found her in the morning room. After a few idle observations about the looks of the estate, he asked, "Eugenia, have you ever considered pensioning Nanny off?"

She looked up. "Oh, dear, yes. However, I think she's too old ever to take on another post but she still likes to feel useful, so we won't take any action for the present."

"Are you aware of her hostility toward Miss Windom?"

She frowned. "You know she always considers her charges as her own children. I think that feeling is even stronger in Delphie's case, because she doubtless realizes she'll never have another infant to raise. Then, too, she had almost the sole care of Delphie last year when Claire was ill. I'm afraid I neglected the other children sadly. I suspect Nanny resents seeing Jessica assume authority that she feels belongs to her."

"And does Miss Windom usurp Nanny's authority?"

"Not in general. I think she tries to stay out of purely nursery matters. But there was one instance when she first came—there was a contest of wills between the two, and I had to side with Jessica. I suppose Nanny felt it keenly. Jessica could have been more tactful, but she saw something that needed doing so she did it. She's very direct. It was something I should have seen for myself, but sometimes an outsider sees a situation more clearly."

"Twice now Nanny has tried to feed me poisoned tales—quite unfounded—about Miss Windom," he said.

"Oh, dear, I *am* sorry. But I shouldn't think she'll try it with me. And if she did, I would recognize that it was founded in spite. Have no fear—I recognize Jessica for the treasure she is, and the girls are devoted to her. Nanny knows that. Perhaps she was just trying to secure one other person to share her ill opinion, and she chose you. Actually we go on quite harmoniously."

"I'm happy there is no real problem," he said.

"Speaking of problems, I should warn you, perhaps," his sister said. "The girls have been promised the high treat of taking tea with their adored Uncle Robert."

"That will be a high treat for their adoring uncle," he retorted, dropping an affectionate kiss on her cheek, and went upstairs to change out of his riding clothes.

The school party arrived for tea, scrubbed and glowing, Claire in primrose, Delphie in white with a pink sash. Their governess, in a prim, high-necked cambric gown of suitably dull blue, managed to look scarcely older than Claire.

"Oh, uncle, we want to show you our collections!" Delphie said enthusiastically.

"I will be glad to see them," he said, "so long as they don't jump at me like the twins' toads."

"Those were frogs, not toads," Claire corrected, giggling.

"Well, when anything leaps so far and furiously, it can't expect me to be able to identify its species properly," he returned.

"Our specimens don't jump, but they *are* savage," Delphie said, "because they're *wild*flowers."

Her uncle broke into laughter and tossed her triumphantly into the air. "Is Miss Windom giving you courses in witticisms, child?"

Jessica promptly said, "Not at all. The remark was all her own," but it was easy to see that she was proud of her pupil's quickness.

When the wildflower collection had been duly admired, Delphie said, "Now we're beginning on mosses. How many of these can you name, Uncle?"

"This one is Elizabeth, and here is Alfrida, and this one over here is Adeline," he said solemnly.

"Oh, do be serious, Uncle Robert. Can't you name any of them?" Claire chided.

He shrugged. "Well, what's in a name?" Then he pointed at random. "This is an attractive one. Is it very rare?"

Delphie laughed. "That's silvery bryum and it's *very* common."

"I'm shocked to hear it. It looks quite well bred," he said, and they dissolved into laughter. "I fear, however, that moss has never been my forte."

"You should take an interest, Uncle," Claire admonished him. "They are very interesting. Pliny the Elder used the term *bryum* way back in the first century. And do you know what moss appears on a royal coat of arms?"

"I'm afraid I don't," he admitted meekly, "but I'm sure you'll enlighten me."

"Knight's plume or *Hypnum cristacastrensis* appears

on the arms of the House of Lancaster," she said triumphantly.

"Dear me, you make me wish to go straight out and start gathering moss, but unfortunately I am a rolling stone and therefore cannot do so but must roll on to Ashendene instead."

"You will come back for our ball, though, will you not?" Claire asked anxiously. "Mama has said that I may attend in the early hours."

"I would not dream of missing such an event," he assured her solemnly.

"And now we must go back to the schoolroom, girls," Jessica said, rising. "Perhaps, Claire, you would like to take for your Italian lesson your uncle's apt quotation, *pietra mossa non fa muschio*. A rolling stone gathers no moss." And with a sidelong look at the viscount which held an irrepressible gleam, she led her charges out of the room.

Chapter Seven

The Harewoods observed the felicitous tradition of holding a ball each year to mark the anniversary of their marriage, and as this took place in September, it was always the first neighborhood ball of the autumn. Their friends had learned to anticipate not only good food, good company, and good music, but also clement weather, for somehow it never rained on the day of the Harewoods' ball.

As the day approached, Claire experienced a divergence of emotions, for while she was happy on the one hand to be allowed to appear at the ball, she thought it too lowering that she would only be able to stay for the early hours; and while she was pleased with her new dress (though she had at first made a token protest against pink French muslin as "insipid" and opted for a dashing celestial blue crepe), she was disappointed that she would not be allowed to put her hair up nor to wear any jewelry save for a simple necklet of small pearls that had belonged to her mama when she was a girl. In short, she was feeling as capricious as any other young girl on the point of taking her first thrilling yet frightening steps toward adulthood.

As for Jessica, she could not quell a small flicker of excitement, either, for it would be her first appearance at a ball, too, as she was expected to chaperone Claire. She had written to Lady Sarah to apprise her of the splendid preparations for the event and to express gratitude for her friend's foresight in insisting on providing her with a suitable dress.

The house was overflowing with company down from London, and at nearly the last moment the dowager Viscountess Markham had found herself able to attend also. She often did come to stay at Harewood Hall at the time of the anniversary balls, but this year she had been favored by a visit of uncertain duration from one of her late husband's aunts, and it was only at a late date that the aunt had decided to terminate her stay at Ashendene in order to take the waters at Bath, thus freeing Lady Markham from further duty as hostess.

She had not been long in the house before she sought out Jessica to inquire how she was going on, and to present her with a gift that Lady Sarah had sent her, which proved to be a very daintily chased gold bangle to wear to the ball.

Jessica's face lit with pleasure at her friend's thoughtfulness. "I am so happy to see you," she told Lady Markham, "because I welcome the opportunity to thank you again for your kindness in recommending me to Lady Harewood. She is goodness itself, and I enjoy your granddaughters very much."

"Does that mean they provide a special challenge?" Lady Harewood asked with a gleam of amusement.

Jessica's lips twitched. "One would not wish one's work made *too* easy," she answered.

"Well, I understand from my daughter that the thanks for your recommendation are on her side."

On the night of the ball, Jessica stayed away from Claire's room while the girl dressed because Nanny had made it clear that the finishing touches to her babe's appearance were her special province.

Rose came to Jessica, bringing a tiny knot of yellow rosebuds she had fashioned to pin in her hair. The green silk, though it was of a subdued shade, had a rich, shimmering sheen to it; and though it was cut modestly, still it showed Jessica's slender neck and delicately rounded arms to advantage. She wore her locket and the gold bangle, and with the twist of yellow flowers in her dark curls, Rose pronounced her a fair treat to look at.

"Will there be enough refreshments for the staff," Jessica asked, "or shall I smuggle some cakes to you?"

"Oh, there'll be cakes aplenty," Rose said, "but Cook won't ever let us have any of the lobster patties. I've always fancied one."

"Well, you shall have mine," Jessica promised conspiratorially just as Claire appeared at the door, fairly dancing with excitement. Jessica and Rose both pronounced the new dress a great success, though the governess did caution her charge that it was *not* considered the crack of fashion for a lady of polite society to bounce around like an India rubber ball.

As they descended the staircase, it seemed as if the whole county were assembled below. "Oh, let us slow down," Claire whispered. "There is his Grace the Duke of Salford, who is the highest ranking personage here tonight. Wait until he passes on into the other room, as I don't want to have to make my first curtsy tonight to a *duke*."

"He does not look so very alarming," Jessica said.

But Claire answered, "His manner is very odd and abrupt though, and I do so want to be a credit to you, which I will not be if I go off into a fit of the giggles or of stammering."

"I agree that would be a lamentable beginning to your career in society," Jessica laughed.

She had no reason to be ashamed of Claire, as that young lady showed a very pretty blend of poise and modesty.

Since Jessica of course did not put herself forward by entering into conversations, what she enjoyed most was watching the dancing. At one point Lady Harewood, looking quite beautiful in amber satin under blonde lace, came to say, "Miss Windom, my mother is over in the far alcove talking to an old friend of hers, and she would like to have Claire come and join them for half an hour. She is very proud of you, my love," she smiled at Claire. "You may leave her there and enjoy yourself for a while. Please dance, if you wish, my dear," she said to Jessica.

After delivering her charge into her grandmother's keeping, Jessica was moving quietly around the perimeter of the room when through a doorway in front of her stepped a figure she recognized as the Duke of

Salford, whom Claire had pointed out earlier. He was quite tall, with a creased, ruddy face, bushy white eyebrows, and splendidly piercing blue eyes.

He stopped at the sight of her. "Have I not met you before?" he inquired rather fiercely.

She dropped a curtsy. "No, your Grace. I'm the Harewood girls' governess."

"What's your name?"

"Jessica Windom, your Grace."

"Governess, eh," he mused. "You look too young. Good bones, too. Not bookish, are you?" His tone made it an accusation.

Her eyes twinkled as she confessed demurely, "I'm afraid I am."

"Oh, well then, might as well be a governess in that case. Thought you might be a noblewoman fallen on hard times and had to take up a job because your father gambled away his fortune. Read something like it in a rubbishy novel once—that is to say, my daughter-in-law read it to me when I was laid up with the gout. Couldn't stop her."

An amused chuckle escaped her lips. "No, my case was nothing like that. I had no higher expectations than teaching, and indeed my situation is so agreeable here that I could never think of it as falling upon hard times."

"Sure I haven't met you before?"

"No, your Grace, though perhaps you might have seen me once or twice trespassing in your woods, though I certainly tried to remain unobserved," she said frankly.

"Eh? Not poaching, were you?"

"Not precisely. Though I was extremely tempted to carry away something that belongs to you. Only the very sternest reminders to myself of the Reverend Mr. Raynes's sermons on honesty held me back."

"And what was that you wanted to steal from me?" he demanded.

"There's a patch of *buxbaumia aphylla* in your north wood. I greatly coveted a sample for my specimen box, but I *very* nobly refrained from gathering any, which almost makes me wish I didn't revere Mr. Raynes's scruples so highly."

"What's that you say? *Buxbaumia aphylla* moss? In my woods? You may be bookish, but you can't know much about mosses. I've been collecting them for fifty years and I've never found any *buxbaumia*."

"I did not know you were a botanist, your Grace, but I must disagree with you. There is *buxbaumia aphylla* in your woods."

"You show it to me and I'll—I'll buy you a pair of diamond eardrops."

"I'll be very happy to show you the moss whenever you choose, your Grace."

"Then we'll make it tomorrow. And the eardrops will be yours by the end of the week."

"Certainly not," she said reprovingly. "I scarcely need a reward for pointing out your own moss to you."

"Be well worth it," he said. "It would cap my collection."

"But you must see that I couldn't accept such a gift," she said.

He stared at her, then gave a great bark of laughter.

"Oh, propriety, is it? Well, you're quite out there. Been a widower for thirty years. No one could be such a clunch as to think I was casting out lures at my age. Not that you're not a well-looking gal. Not a beauty, but you've got countenance. Diamonds would set you off to advantage."

"But you see, as a governess, I couldn't wear them. It would be quite ineligible."

Jessica was so engrossed in the conversation that she had no notion that half the room was watching and wondering how a governess had managed to hold the duke at her side for so long. When he had suddenly exploded in laughter, curiosity threatened to overcome them all. One guest, Lord Markham, apparently *was* overcome by it, for he strolled up, looking the very picture of elegance in his superbly cut black coat and white satin waistcoat. A ruby stickpin, his only ornament, glowed in the fold of his intricately tied cravat.

"Good evening, your Grace."

"Hallo, Robert. Haven't seen you since Whitsuntide. Suppose I don't need to introduce you to Miss Windom if she's your nieces' governess."

"Yes, we are acquainted," he said with a little bow to Jessica.

"Bookish, she tells me," the duke confided. "Foolish chit, though. Just been trying to tell me I mustn't give her diamond eardrops."

The viscount gave a visible start of surprise.

With an amiable wave to both of them, the duke moved off.

The viscount looked expectantly at Jessica, confident that she would explain Salford's mystifying words about diamond eardrops. If she recognized the look for what it was, she ignored it. "This is a lovely ball, is it not?"

"Yes, my sister is a most accomplished hostess. Everyone seems to enjoy her parties, even the Duke of Salford, and he rarely accepts invitations. He seems in prime humor tonight."

Still she did not rise to the bait, though she herself would have been hard pressed to explain why. "Delphie and Claire were so pleased that Lady Markham could come. They are hoping she will make a lengthy stay."

Somewhat exasperated that in spite of her intellectual pretensions, Miss Windom did not seem to understand that in polite conversation some questions should be answered without their having to be asked, the viscount decided that Miss Windom might be more forthcoming on the dance floor and said to her, "May I request the honor of leading you out?"

She looked startled. "Oh, you're very kind, but I am here only as Claire's chaperone."

"But as Claire is seated with my mama at the moment, that hardly constitutes a hindrance."

"What I meant was that I do not intend to dance."

"But surely you could be persuaded to change your mind."

"I think not, thank you."

She was being so dignified and governessy, and all the while looking like a schoolgirl at her first party, that he was prompted to say, "Oh, how clumsy of me.

They're playing a waltz. And of course having been taught in a vicarage, you don't know how to waltz."

Taking affront, she began impulsively, "I *do* know how—" and then bit her lip in annoyance.

"In that case," he said, and brooking no further objection, swept her onto the floor.

How different it was to be caught up in the swirl of dancers than to be a spectator, she thought. They revolved beneath the crystal chandeliers to the lilting music, Lord Markham's arm firmly encircling her waist and guiding her so that she did not even have to think about how to follow his steps.

She looked up at him and remembered how the first time he had ever spoken to her he was riding a great white horse. She had been so ashamed to be seen because she was wearing trousers and sitting astride a horse of her cousin's without his permission, and she was a little afraid, too. But Lord Markham had given her *such* a smile and told her not to worry, that he would keep her secret. And now here she was actually *waltzing* with him and wearing a pretty dress, too, and flowers in her hair.

For just a short breadth of time, she wondered what it would be like to belong in such a setting, to be a carefree girl looking forward to a whole season of balls and glittering raiment and morning calls from gentlemen—to be someone like that tall, very fair girl in the white dress with diamante trim with whom she had watched Lord Markham waltz earlier. Miss Henderson was tall enough by tilting her head only a very little to look into his eyes as they danced, instead of into the folds of his cravat. Perhaps on the whole it was as well that she herself was so short of stature that he couldn't see her eyes.

She was feeling almost giddy when the music ended. He thanked her formally, and at her request took her back to his mother and Claire.

Early the next afternoon, dressed in riding clothes, Lord Markham strolled into the library to return a book and with some little surprise saw that his brother-in-law was its sole occupant. "I didn't expect to find you here alone, John," and at the questioning rise of Lord Harewood's brows went on, "That is, my man mentioned that he had seen the duke's carriage drive up a short time ago."

"Yes; he didn't come to see me though. Funny thing, that. Eugenia says he sent a footman over with a note this morning asking if Miss Windom could be spared for an hour to drive out with him. Of course she gave permission, but it's a queer start, what?"

The viscount murmured some random remark and made his way to the stables, a frown creasing his brow.

Chevron was in prime form, eager for a gallop, and at the end of twenty minutes or so, the crisp sunny air had worked some tonic effect on his master. Then as he passed across the field skirting the Salford woods, he saw the duke's carriage standing still on the road. It was of old-fashioned design and a peculiar mustard shade which he would have recognized even had he not been able to identify the distinctive blue and red emblazonment on the panel.

His first thought was that there might be some trouble, but a second look showed him the coachman sitting calmly on the box.

For reasons he could hardly have explained, it would have embarrassed him to have the occupants of the carriage see him, as if he were spying on them, so he wheeled Chevron toward the woods and plunged into the sheltering cover, slowing the horse to a walk. It was not many minutes before he realized with dismay that the path he had taken was the most unfortunate of all possible choices, for there ahead of him, walking with their backs to him, were the duke and Miss Windom, she in a dark-colored mantle, so tiny her head scarcely reached the shoulder of the tall, straight figure of the old duke.

The viscount swore softly and checked Chevron. What a fool he was! If it would have looked odd for him to have passed their carriage, how much worse, a thousand times worse, to seem to have followed them into the woods. He would wait until they had gone a distance farther, then very quietly turn Chevron and with luck ride away unnoticed.

But suddenly the two figures stopped, and then, before the viscount's astonished eyes, the Duke of Salford had gone down on his knees before Miss Windom.

Blindly he turned Chevron and plunged back through the wood, disregarding any noise he might make.

It was an odd conflict of emotions that beset him as he rode back to Harewood Hall. Little Miss Windom—what was it she was to be, a duchess, or a duke's mistress? Since his wife died, there had never been any gossip that Salford was in the petticoat line. Very likely it was marriage he was proposing. Markham felt he should be happy for her—it would be one in the eye for those cheese-paring, scaley relations of hers. She would never have to worry about earning her bread again, would be able to command all the elegancies of life. But the duke was seventy and Miss Windom—well, she was nothing but a child.

His mind shrank in distaste from the thought of the laughter and coarse talk that would echo around the county. "Poor old Salford, caught in a parson's mousetrap—leg-shackled to a governess. She took a lucky tumble into the cream pot."

He spurred Chevron onward, circling far beyond Harewood Hall until the two of them were exhausted before finally turning back to the house. In the stable yard a half-dozen of the guests who had come down for the ball were just mounting up for a ride, but he spoke to none of them beyond a mechanical greeting.

He entered the house by way of a side door, but as he crossed the hall to the staircase, the butler was just ushering in the duke and Miss Windom. Once more the viscount cursed his timing, but there was no way short of insult to avoid a confrontation.

"Ho there, Markham," the duke said, beaming. "Been for a ride, I see. Splendid day for it."

"Good day, your Grace. Miss Windom," he said colorlessly.

"Been for a drive myself," the old man went on, his ruddy face alive with enthusiasm. "A very successful outing. This gal is a smart 'un, you know that?"

There was an uncomfortable pause, and then the viscount said carefully, "I have for some time been aware of Miss Windom's powers of intellect."

"Aware of my intellectual pretensions, is the way I should have thought you would put it," she said with a little gurgle of laughter.

"Didn't think so at first. Suspected she didn't know her toe from her topknot, but she proved me wrong. You see me a very happy man, Markham."

"I wish you both very happy," the viscount said stiffly.

"Well, and so we are. Just what I was telling you. Show him, my dear."

The viscount had been careful not to look at Jessica's face, for he didn't know what he would read there: smugness, triumph? Now he did turn his eyes to her and saw her much as usual, the heart-shaped mouth calm above her firm little chin, but perhaps an extra sparkle in the clear gray eyes.

His glance dropped to the box she was holding. It was far too big for a ring, large enough for a tiara. He would not have thought she would have sold herself for a tiara, but a duchess's coronet—perhaps that was a temptation beyond resisting.

She lifted the lid and he half-shut his eyes against the flash of gems he expected to see, and then, blinking, looked again.

"Old *leaves*!" he exclaimed in a odd voice.

"Old leaves indeed!" She sounded affronted but there was amusement in her face. "You can't have been paying proper attention when your nieces showed you their moss collection."

91

"*Buxbaumia aphylla*," the duke said, rolling the words in a pleased manner on his tongue. "And in my own woods. Gathered it with my own hands. But it took this gal's sharp eyes to find it. First bookish miss I ever knew with good sense. Except about the eardrops. Not showing sense there. Ought to have them. Offer still stands."

"No, thank you, your Grace. I'm more than repaid by your giving me this specimen of the *buxbaumia*—without my having to poach it," she added impishly.

"No use saying the *buxbaumia* ain't more interesting than diamonds, because it is, but a young chit like you ought to have diamonds too. Set you off to a nicety. Make you seem less bookish. Might attract you a husband. Then you could give up all this bookish business."

She flushed rather rosily, but laughed and shook her head firmly. "Bookish business suits me very well, your Grace."

Disappointed, he took her hand and dropped a courtly kiss on her fingertips. "I'll say good-bye then, my dear. And mind, you can walk in my woods whenever you wish."

She curtsied and turned to run lightly up the stairs to her charges. "Nice gal," the duke commented. "Stubborn, though. Like to give her a present. Wonder if she'd like a parrot. Or a monkey. Remember my granddaughter was mad to have a monkey once."

"I've never heard Miss Windom express a desire for a monkey," his lordship said, straining to keep his countenance. "And I'm not sure my brother-in-law would be pleased to have one in the house."

"Eh? What affair is it of his? Well, yes, it is his house, I suppose," the duke admitted grudgingly. "Worst of being a governess. Have to ask permission to keep a monkey. Bad business, this bookishness. See where it leads."

He took his leave of Lord Markham and went off to his carriage and his *buxbaumia*, whereupon the viscount repaired to the library and, quite contrary to his usual afternoon habits, drank a rather large glass of brandy.

Chapter Eight

September melted into October. Lady Markham had returned to Ashendene, and the ball was only a pleasant memory.

The Harewood girls continued to apply themselves properly to their studies at least for a good share of the time; the twins alternately played pranks and appealed to Jessica for help with last-minute cramming sessions; Jemmy's progress filled her with pride even though she was disappointed that Lord Markham had not as yet found any suitable solution to the problem of his education. Though he had written her a note telling of several schools he had looked into, none of them had seemed to fit the bill. She suspected he didn't take the matter as seriously as he might.

One day just as Jessica and the girls were on the point of repairing to the schoolroom after luncheon, Rose came with the message that there was a gentleman asking to see her who said he was her cousin, and that Lady Harewood had had him shown to the morning room.

There was annoyance in her face as she sent the girls upstairs and went reluctantly to meet him. He was standing with his back to the door, but turned as he heard her step and advanced toward her, holding out both hands to clasp hers as he bent over to touch his lips to her fingertips.

Suppressing a shudder of distaste, she repossessed herself of her hands as quickly as possible. "Well, Harry, it's quite a surprise to see you."

"But not, I trust, an unpleasant one, as were the two bitter surprises I received when I arrived home to find my father deceased and my family dispersed."

"You have my condolences on the death of your father, but as for the rest—your sisters have resided away from Gray Gables for some years and you never cared for Cousin Frances, so I do not see how you could have found that part so very bitter," she remarked reasonably.

He gave her an aggrieved look. "But for *you* to desert me, Jessie, that was quite something else."

She could not imagine why he was adopting such a false pose. He had never been inclined to play the gallant before. In looks he had not changed. He was tall, broad-faced, carrying a little too much weight even for his heavy-boned frame. His complexion was ruddy, his hair dark. His harsh-featured face would have looked strong had it not been for his eyes, which were a surprisingly pale, watery blue under short and scanty lashes.

"Desertion is not an apt word, Harry. There was no one left at Gray Gables for me to desert. And even had your father lived, I would not have remained there much longer. I have my way to make in the world."

"Jessie, you hurt me to the quick. *Your way to make*, indeed! Surely you know that Gray Gables will always be your home."

"Commendably charitable, Harry," she said drily, "but quite unnecessary. I have a good position here in which I can be useful."

"Don't speak to me of charity," he said. "You cannot help but know that it has always been intended that you should be my wife."

He could not have astonished her more. She felt staggered by this revelation. "Have your wits quite gone begging?" she asked. "*Intended!* The thought never crossed my mind—nor yours either."

"It was my father's deathbed wish, which I should feel honor-bound to carry out even if it were not the project nearest my own heart, but I assure you that it is."

At this she burst out laughing. "You were nowhere near your father's deathbed, Harry, and he certainly never expressed such a wish to me. Had he done so, I would have recommended that he had better think of a different deathbed wish, because that is one which I shall certainly never carry out."

His jaw hardened. "He gave you a home, the very food in your mouth, and you wouldn't do the one little thing he asked of you?"

"He *didn't* ask it, Harry. I cannot think he meant for his precious son to marry a base-born brat, as he so charitably pointed out was my condition."

"You were dearer to him than you realized," he persisted. "And you must believe it was his earnest intention that we wed."

"I should not have thought you so vulnerable, Harry, but I believe that grief has disordered your mind. Even if what you say were true, it is not my intention to marry you, nor will it ever be." She rose and rang for the butler. "I must get back to my work now, Harry. The children are waiting for their lessons."

"I cannot take this as final," he said. "If you truly did not divine my father's wishes—and mine—then I have taken you by surprise. When you have had time to reflect, you will find that you feel quite differently. I will give you time, and then I will return for a favorable reply."

"Never, Harry, not if you gave me a hundred years. Do not waste your time by coming again." And then to the butler, "Mr. Broyles was just leaving." She waited in the hall until the door closed behind Harry, then said, "If the gentleman should call again, Mason, I'm not at home to him."

She mounted the staircase in a state of total bewilderment. It was not in the least in his character to have come to see for himself whether she was comfortably situated. It was all most puzzling.

The following days were warm and sunny. Jessica and the girls were returning from a walk one day, still some little distance down the drive from the house, when they heard horses behind them and stepped off onto the grass. Instead of passing on, the vehicle drew to a stop beside them. To Jessica's annoyance, she saw it was Harry driving a curricle with a pair of prime goers.

"You again," she said with a frown.

"Come now, Jessie, I thought you'd be happier to see me than that. It was not easy to contrive. The old fish-face up at the house wouldn't let me in."

"On my orders, Harry. I have nothing to say to you."

"But I have a great deal to say to you, only I hadn't thought it would be best said in front of the children. Come for a drive with me."

"No, Harry."

His face turned ugly. "Well, you can't stop me from driving along beside you and saying—oh, maybe lots of things not suitable for young ears. Or maybe the little kiddie would like to go for a ride with me," he looked at Delphie and made as if to jump down from the curricle. She shrank back against Jessica.

"Let her alone, I warn you." Jessica's voice was sharp.

"Then come for a little drive. That's all I ask. Just a chance to have my say—is that so much for a cousin to ask?"

She hesitated. "Very well, a short drive. Take Delphie up to the house, Claire. Go to the schoolroom and start your lessons. I'll be along presently."

He helped her into the curricle and turned the horses expertly. He caught his thong neatly and they set off at a brisk pace. One thing that could be said for Harry—he was an expert whip.

"Harry, I'm sorry you put yourself to the trouble of coming here again. I meant what I said before. I won't change my mind."

"Jessie, Jessie, you can't have thought the matter

through. You'll be mistress of Gray Gables. You can even hire some more servants. You'll have your own carriage, and pretty clothes, and standing in the community. How can you not prefer such an agreeable fate to being a servant in someone else's house?"

"There's no disgrace in working for a living, if you give value for your pay. I enjoy my work."

"But would you not enjoy having your own home more?"

"Not at this price," she said evenly. "Admit it, Harry, we wouldn't suit."

He whipped up the horses. She looked at him, his mouth set in an ugly line, and shivered. The very thought of being tied for life to such a one filled her with disgust. All the pretty speeches he had made when he had called on her before—that was not the real Harry speaking. The real Harry was the one who had frightened the children back on the drive, the one who was now lashing his horses in fury, the one who had always turned ugly if his will was crossed.

He would run the horses till his anger had worn itself thin, and then it would not at all surprise her if he put her down by the side of the road and made her walk home alone. Well, if he did, at least she would be in better company, she reflected. The only odd thing was why had he taken this maggot into his head about marrying her in the first place.

Could it be that he merely had decided it was time to take a wife, someone to run Gray Gables, and he had considered her meek enough and enough accustomed to taking orders that she would let him go his own way with never a thought of crossing him? Poor

Cousin Jessie with no prospects, no name even—she would have to be grateful for any crust he threw to her and would never dream of denying his most unreasonable whim. Was that what he thought?

The problem was that the meek, obedient Jessie he had always seen was not the real Jessica either. It was only the face she had chosen to wear in that household, knowing that her safety lay in going unnoticed.

"Harry," she said at last in a voice carefully devoid of emotion, "your team is tired. Turn them now and take me home."

At length he turned to her, his lips curled in a sneer. "But we aren't going back, my dear wife-to-be. We're going to the Red Hare, where I've engaged a room for us."

"Don't play the fool, Harry," she said evenly. "You know I wouldn't go to an inn with you."

"You haven't any choice. The arrangements are made. I had hoped you'd be sensible enough to make it pleasant for yourself, but since you haven't, we'll have to do it the hard way. Because I will have you, Jessie, make no mistake."

A flicker of fear ran through her, but she said, "Not as your wife, Harry. Never as your wife."

"Oh, I think so. You'll be glad enough to marry me in the end, because I'll ruin you. We're going to spend the night together, my dear cousin."

She swallowed back the revulsion that surged in her throat to say levelly, "You can ruin me, Harry, but I tell you plainly: I will never marry you."

"No one else will have you—after tonight."

"I've never counted my chances of marrying very

high, and I would rather go through life as a ruined woman than as your wife."

"Fine talk, but how will you live, Cousin?" he mocked. "Tomorrow, or maybe one day next week, I'll send a note to your grand employers at Harewood Hall to tell them that you ran away with your lover. Do you think they'd have you back? You? A fallen woman—to have the care of their precious daughters?"

For just a moment she felt a little faint. Then she said, "I doubt they'd believe you, but if they did, then I would go back to the Raynes's, because they know me well, Harry, and they know you, and they would never take your word against me."

He laughed softly. "And your child, Jessie. If you should have a child, would they take in the bastard too, and rear it?"

She was shaking with anger now. "You can complicate my life and blacken my reputation, but I swear to you, whatever happens I'll be no wife to you—ever!"

"You'll come to your senses," Harry said. "And I begin to think I will enjoy this honeymoon—you being so spirited and all—more than I had expected. There will be more sport in it this way."

"You're loathsome," she said with deep repugnance. He made her feel physically ill, but she knew she must not give in to weakness. Her mind was already moving ahead. When they entered the Red Hare, she would beg protection from the landlord at once, embarrassing as it would be.

"And don't think to try any tricks, miss," he said. "You may think you're awake on every suit being a governess and all, but don't try to cross wits with Harry Broyles, because he's two steps ahead of an innocent like you."

She did not even ask what he meant, so intent was she on what she would say to the landlord, how she would contrive to return to Harewood Hall with the least fuss, when suddenly she sensed an odd movement and was just turning her head when she felt a stunning blow at the base of her skull and the world went black.

The blackness was so kind, easing her aching head, that she wished to be allowed to sink back into it. She tried to escape the annoyance of the cold, wet thing pressed to her forehead. Then she felt a burning in her nostrils which spread down into her lungs, and she choked and opened her eyes.

The ceiling swung in an arc above her, steadied, and then she saw a worried face, which was somehow familiar, bent close to her own. "Oh, you're awake, miss!"

She struggled to sit up; faintness overcame her momentarily, and a cool cloth was pressed to her face again. The blackness receded, and she opened her eyes again and looked at the girl in the white cap holding a vinaigrette in one hand and a damp handkerchief in the other.

Jessica frowned, trying to remember. "I know you, don't I? You're—you're—"

"Rose's sister, Lucy. Rose Cauley, up to Harewood Hall, miss."

"Of course. Lucy. I remember now. You came to see Rose once. I'm Jessica Windom, the governess."

"Yes, miss. I recognized you. I was that surprised when Mr. Broyles carried you in."

Harry! She sat up with a start, then clutched her head as pain throbbed anew. She looked wildly around the room and with relief saw that she was lying in a small private parlor, a corner room with windows on two sides, and out of the windows she could see that it was on the ground floor.

"How long have I been here?" she asked, trembling.

"Just a few minutes, miss. Mr. Broyles was *that* angry when he found your room wasn't ready, but the gentleman what had the room last night, being a trifle castaway, if you take my meaning, slept half the day away, and since Mr. Broyles never said what time to expect you, and the other gentleman being a good customer and all, Mr. Crawford didn't hardly like to wake him and put him out. So they put you in here and now Mr. Broyles is out in the taproom having a pint."

"Mr. Crawford is the landlord?" Lucy nodded. "Send him to me at once. He must help me to get away. Harry Broyles has kidnapped me."

Lucy's eyes grew wide. "Oh, *miss*!"

"I must get back to Harewood Hall. The landlord can surely provide me with some sort of transportation."

Lucy was twisting the handkerchief in her hands and said unhappily, "I shouldn't think he'd do that, miss. You see, Mr. Broyles has been staying here three nights now. Very friendly he's become with Mr. Crawford, standing him to brandy and spending very free. He told Mr. Crawford he was bringing his bride here today after the wedding and bespoke the best bedroom."

"Did Mr. Crawford not think it odd that the 'bride' should have been bashed into unconsciousness?" Jessica asked astringently.

"Mr. Broyles said it was too much champagne what did you in—at the wedding party."

"Well, I'll simply explain it to him if you'll fetch him, Lucy."

"But miss," the girl protested miserably, "I don't think it will do any good. You see, he told Mr. Crawford that the two of you had been engaged and then you fancied yourself in love with a soldier. Wanted to run off with him, you did. Your dad was fearful you'd ruin yourself so he married you out of hand to your intended. So if you go to cutting up a rumpus, Mr. Crawford will only think you're trying to get away from your lawful husband to join your lover, because that's what Mr. Broyles said to expect. He won't lift a finger to help you. Mr. Broyles warned him you might be a little difficult—till you was halter-broke, he said."

Jessica's eyes had narrowed to angry slits. Through clenched teeth she said, "There's not a word of truth in it."

"No, miss. I believe you. Rose sets a heap of store by you. But I don't know what's to do."

"Is there no one besides Mr. Crawford to turn to? His wife? Other travelers?"

Lucy shook her head. "He has no wife and there's no one staying here besides you at the moment but a couple of commercial travelers, and Mr. Broyles is out there standing them drinks and telling them about the wedding. They won't interfere, and the other servants wouldn't dare to cross Mr. Crawford."

Jessica looked at her in dismay, then took a firm grip on herself. "Could you give me paper and a pen, then, Lucy? I must send a note to Harewood Hall. There must be someone to carry it."

"Well," the girl said, "I guess I could get the ostler's boy to do it. I've smuggled food to him more than one night when his dad punished him by sending him to bed hungry. He's a high-spirited lad, which gets him into trouble, but he's one to take a risk. I think he'd do it for me."

Jessica quickly set about writing the note. It was to be delivered to the Harewood stables, as she did not want to involve anyone at the house in such a sordid business. The head groom or Jemmy's father should be able to deal with Harry. They could certainly put the lie to Harry's story about a wedding and her dad marrying her out of hand, if it should be necessary to inlist Mr. Crawford to her aid.

Lucy slipped out with the note, and Jessica settled back to wait. She considered escaping through the window, but upon arising and trying to walk briskly about the room, her throbbing head warned her that she was too weak to run effectively. There was no way she could walk all the distance back to Harewood in this condition, and if she were hiding in a hedgerow when her rescuer arrived, it would only delay her return home. More likely Harry would miss her and overtake her before she had had time to get far.

Her reflections were interrupted by the opening of the door. "Well, my dear, I see you are awake," came the hateful voice. "You must let me help you up the stairs, as Mr. Crawford informs me that our room is ready at last."

"Aren't you forgetting something, Harry?" she asked loudly, approaching the door. "We haven't had our luncheon."

"It's past time for lunch," he said, lazily amused. "Come, let us go up."

She came out of the parlor and stood where she could be seen and heard by the two commercial travelers and the landlord. "Then we shall have high tea or supper or whatever Mr. Crawford cares to call it. But I have not had a bite to eat all day, being far too nervous for breakfast, and I am famished. I make no doubt that whatever the hour, this good landlord will be willing to provide a bridal meal." She looked appealingly at Mr. Crawford.

He had been warned she might be difficult and he had hoped this difficulty would not involve broken crockery. A simple request for food did not seem beyond the line. He nodded.

Jessica gazed thoughtfully into space. "I believe . . . that what I fancy . . . is a nice poached capon."

"Well, ma'am," he said, "I'm afraid there is no capon poached at the moment."

"Then poach one," she said.

"That's nonsense," Harry said irritably. "Some sandwiches will do us fine."

She rounded on him. "*Sandwiches!* Sandwiches? Is this the man who only this morning promised to cherish me, to cater to my every desire, to give me the sun and the moon? And now you offer me *sandwiches* for my bridal meal?"

The commercial travelers turned away to hide their broad grins.

"I'm sure a poached capon is not so much to ask, do you think, Mr. Crawford? After all, unless some untimely accident of fate should remove you from this earth before me, Harry," she said with an ironic glint in her eyes, "then this will be the only wedding luncheon I shall ever have, and I shall have poached capon or not budge a foot."

"I'll see to it right away, ma'am," Mr. Crawford said.

Harry led Jessica back into the parlor. "You're very clever, aren't you?" he asked, sneering. "But delaying things will make no difference in the long run."

"I'm hungry, Harry," she said. "Since we have our whole lifetime ahead of us, why begin it on an empty stomach?"

He grinned. "True; we have a whole lifetime," he said, and went out to order another pint.

When Lucy returned and gave her a conspirator's nod, she went to tidy up, taking Lucy with her. "The note is on its way, miss," she whispered.

"Fine. Now we're going to have a meal presently, and when you serve, be as slow as you can. And be sure to keep Harry's wineglass filled."

"Oh, yes, miss. I only wish I had some poison to drop into it."

* * *

Eventually the bird was served, tender and succulent, surrounded with vegetables. Though her headache had diminished considerably, Jessica was not interested in food. However, she forced herself to make a meal, taking dainty bites and chewing with deliberation. Hopeful as every minute ticked by that she would soon be hearing a commotion at the door which betokened the arrival of her rescuer, she ate as slowly as she could. But by the time her plate was empty, that happy event had not occurred, so she thought of several more delicacies she vowed she could not do without on her wedding day. She was willing to wager that the cook at the Red Hare hadn't had such a challenging day in years.

She was just on the point of deciding she could not eat another morsel to save her life when Harry gave a start and said, "What's that?"

She turned to look at the west window where he pointed and saw with a mixture of dismay and relief that it was one of the twins, his mouth drawn into a grotesque grimace. The message must have reached Harewood Hall, but why was Phillip or Peter here instead of the groom? "I don't see anything," she said blandly and, turning back, saw that the other twin had positioned himself similarly in the south window.

Harry sputtered, "Looks like an imp of Satan. Do you mean you can't see him?"

"There's no one there."

"Eyebrows going up to a point," he insisted, "and a horrible mouth. You *must* see him."

"Oh, *him*. But you're looking at the wrong window.

He's over there," she said, pointing to the south window.

Harry whirled around and choked.

"You must have had too much to drink, Harry. You're seeing double."

He jumped up, letting his chair crash to the floor, and strode over to the window. Meanwhile the twin in the west window disappeared and a moment later slipped quietly in through the door. "I'll get you now, you scoundrel," Harry shouted, trying to raise the sash.

"Harry, you're talking to an empty window. He's behind you now," she said.

He spun from the face in the window to see an identical one in the room with him. His jaw dropped in complete consternation. He advanced toward this demon creature, all his fuddled concentration focused on it, and Jessica snatched up a wine bottle and brought it down on his head with as much force as she could muster.

He dropped like a stone.

Jessica threw her arms around Peter, for it was he in the room. "We came in the pony cart," he said. "I say, this is great fun. Shall we be knocking out anyone else?"

"I hope not," she laughed shakily. "Run out and tell Phillip we'll be leaving in a moment."

She opened the parlor door and, seeing that the coast was clear, whispered to Peter to slip quietly outside and wait for her. A moment later Lucy came into the taproom and Jessica beckoned to her. Pointing to the recumbent Harry, she said, "I've knocked him out and I'm going home now. I can't thank you enough for your help. I could never have managed without you."

"Oh, I'm glad you're safe, miss. And what shall I tell the gentleman when he wakes up?" Lucy inquired. "About what's happened to you, I mean."

Jessica cast a glance of contempt over the untidy, prostrate form of Harry Broyles. "Yes, I suppose he will wake up eventually, worse luck. When he does you can tell him that a *deus ex machina* has carried me off to Olympus."

Lucy's brow wrinkled. "Olympus? Is that over east beyond Shelbyford?"

A hysterical giggle escaped Jessica's lips. "A good deal east of Shelbyford, I'd say." And then as the girl's face held such a puzzled expression, she added, "Oh, look, Lucy, in Greek plays when the hero was in dire straits, a god in a machine would swoop down to the rescue; that's what I meant." She heard one of the twins give a shout that the pony cart was ready. There was only a small coin in her reticule, but she pressed it into Lucy's hand. "This is all I have now, but would you give it to the ostler's boy? I'll come back and see you soon, if I may and bring you a present. I can never thank you enough for your help."

"Oh, miss, no need to thank me. My sister Rose thinks the world and all of you. I couldn't forgive myself if that Mr. Broyles had—"

Jessica interrupted, shuddering, "Yes, I know. Take care now and I'll see you soon."

Chapter Nine

Having enjoyed a leisurely breakfast and a morning riding around the estate with his brother-in-law, the Viscount Markham returned to the house in the expectation of meeting Jessica at luncheon to inquire how she went on. As she was in some part his mother's protégée, he thought he should have a report of her to carry home. However, she did not appear, nor did his sister, so the two men sat down together.

"Where is Eugenia?" the viscount asked after a bit.

"Oh, one of the tenants has a new infant and she has gone to admire it and take it a present," his brother-in-law said carelessly, and Markham did not feel it would be appropriate to ask the whereabouts of the governess.

As the afternoon wore on, the children of the household were conspicuously absent. Eventually the viscount approached the schoolroom door and gave it a brisk knock.

The voice of his elder niece bade him come in. The two girls were sitting quietly at a worktable, and their teacher was not in evidence.

"Hard at your lessons, I see," he commented.

"Yes, Uncle." He thought Claire seemed a little subdued.

"What good, dutiful girls to work so hard with no governess to stand by and scold."

"Miss Windom never scolds," Delphie said defensively.

"Still she should be here to instruct you, shouldn't she?"

Claire's face was worried. "Well, Uncle, I think so too. We thought she'd be back by now."

"Where did she go?"

"In a curricle with a man," Claire brought out. "I'm not perfectly sure she wanted to. We were coming home from our walk when he drove up beside us. He kept asking her to get in and she said no, but then he climbed down and started toward Delphie and said he'd wager the young miss would fancy a ride. But his face had an ugly look and Delphie started to cry. Then Miss Windom agreed to go for a short ride but he was to leave us alone. She told us to run straight into the house and start our lessons and so we did. But if she only went for a *short* ride, she'd be home by now."

The viscount was feeling a faint pricking of alarm. "Did you recognize the man?"

"Oh, yes, he came to see Miss Windom once before. He asked her to marry him and Rose said she sent him away with a flea in his ear."

"To marry him! How do you know that?" he thundered.

"Well, the door was not quite closed and we were in

the next room, Delphie and Rose and I—but only part of the time."

"Listening at the keyhole, I suppose."

"No, just by the crack of the door," she said ingenuously. "She didn't seem to like him at all even though he said he was her cousin."

"Harry Broyles!" Markham exclaimed. "No one else saw him today?"

They shook their heads.

"Are the boys about?"

"No, we heard the pony cart go out about an hour ago. I suppose they were in it."

"Well, you girls continue with your lessons," he said brusquely, and leaving them, he let himself out of the house and strode down to the stables.

The boy Jemmy Dawson was grooming a pretty bay mare. "Do you happen to know where my nephews have gone, Jemmy?" the viscount said.

The browned little face took on a look of consternation. "I suppose they didn't ought to have gone," he said. "Miss's note said not to worry anyone at the house but to send my dad or the undergroom along. Neither of the men were here when the ostler's boy came along though, and the twins were and they read the note and would hear naught but to go theirselves. Me dad ain't back yet. I didn't know what to do."

"The first thing to do, you young rascal, is to tell a straight story. *What* note? Where did they go?"

"To the Red Hare. That's an inn over Landscombe way. The ostler's boy came with a note from Miss—the governess, that is. Said she'd been kidnapped and could me dad come and fetch her. Didn't want to

115

bother the family, she said, but the twins would have it to go theirselves."

"Kidnapped! Not bother the family!" Outrage was evident in every line of the viscount's face. "Get a saddle on Chevron and be quick about it."

Mounted on the huge stallion, he cut across fields to go the shortest way to the Red Hare. The horse was in a sweat when he pounded into the stable yard and fairly threw the reins at the startled boy. Without a word he ran to the door and threw it open.

A startled Lucy, crossing the passageway, dropped a glass at the sight of him, he was so terrible in his anger.

He flung wide the door of a private parlor and strode in, to the astonishment of a plump man and his family who had arrived a short while ago and were partaking of a hearty tea. The wife goggled at him, a piece of cherry cake halfway into her mouth.

"Sir, this parlor is bespoken," the plump man said indignantly.

The viscount's eyes raked the room and, seeing nothing more alarming than the fat-cheeked youngsters chewing bread and butter, he withdrew without a word and rounded on Lucy.

"I am looking for Miss Windom." There was a stern command in his tone.

"Oh, sir, she's already left." Lucy was trembling.

"With—with the man who brought her here?" he choked out.

She cast a nervous glance at the parlor where Harry Broyles lay. The viscount took the cue and opened the door. Harry was still stretched out on the floor.

"What ails him?"

"Well, he's unconscious, you might say," she offered.

"I can see that," was the reply. "Is it drink?"

"Well, he'd been drinking. Miss asked me to keep his glass filled, but it was more the blow on his head laid him out."

"The blow?"

"Could we step in here and speak a little quieter, sir?" she begged. "Mr. Crawford doesn't know miss is gone yet, nor that this one has been struck down, as that other couple with their children came along and distracted him just after she left. Well, I had to help her, of course, but if Mr. Crawford finds out, it might be my job."

Obediently he crossed the threshold and closed the door.

"Are you come from Harewood?" she asked anxiously.

"Yes, my sister is Lady Harewood."

"Well, my sister Rose is a maid there and I'd met Miss Windom once so I recognized her when he carried her in. Seemed a terrible thing, her out cold from too much champagne, such a nice lady and all."

"Champagne!" he barked.

"Well, of course it wasn't that at all, but it was what *he* said," she jerked a thumb at the recumbent Harry. "And the excitement of the wedding, he said. Only there wasn't no wedding nor no champagne neither. He'd hit her over the head. That's what she told me when she came to. Said she'd been abducted and asked me to send a message to the house."

Markham frowned. "I don't understand why she didn't appeal to Crawford."

"Well, not much good it would have done and so I told her. Mr. Broyles had booked a room for himself and his bride yesterday. Got very thick with Mr. Crawford, he did, inviting him to join him in taking brandy. Mr. Crawford doesn't take easily to new ideas. He was expecting a bridal couple and he wouldn't have liked to be told it was a kidnapping instead. Very clever story Mr. Broyles told. The thing was, the room wasn't ready so he had to put her down in here, and Mr. Crawford told me to see to her. That's when she told me what had happened. I sent off the note to the manor, and when Mr. Broyles and the landlord came back, she said she wanted lunch before she went upstairs. Poached capon she fancied, and not a step would she take till she'd eaten. Well, Mr. Crawford could understand that, brides sometimes being notional, so he ordered a capon to be poached and then she asked for a lot of other things—asparagus, jellied veal. Never did I see such a little bit of a lady eat so much. But I kept filling Mr. Broyles's wineglass like she'd asked me to. Lunch went on forever, it seemed like. She's just finished off a fruit tart and sent me for some cheese when it happened."

The viscount had been following this tale with utmost concentration and a peculiar light in his eyes. Now he snapped, "When what happened?"

"I don't rightly know," she confessed, "but when I came in with the cheese, he was lying there and she said he'd been hit on the head and she hoped he'd have a lump the size of a duck egg. And then she left.

118

Said to tell him a Mr. McKenna had taken her over Shelbyford way."

At this revelation the viscount's brow, which had been clearing, clouded over again with bewilderment. "Shelbyford? Why on earth would she go to Shelbyford? And who is Mr. McKenna?"

"Well, I understood her to say he's a Greek gentleman."

"A Greek! With a name like McKenna? Have you lost your wits, girl?"

"I have not," she said, nettled. "I understood her to say that he was an actor chap, so maybe he changed his name. Couldn't expect people to pronounce a Greek name."

"Are you seriously asking me to believe that having escaped her abductor, Miss Windom went off to Shelbyford with a Greek actor named McKenna?" He sounded flabbergasted.

"Well, it wasn't exactly Shelbyford but some village nearby. Olympia, I think. No, Olympus. I couldn't place it precisely, but I thought I'd heard of some such place over east of Shelbyford. I asked her and she said it was a good deal east of there."

He was silent for a moment, and then he said, "Lucy, one more time. Just tell me—in her words— exactly what she said."

Lucy's forehead creased in thought. "She said she supposed *he'd* wake up eventually, worse luck, and if he asked for her I was to say that a Davis X. McKenna had carried her off to Olympus. And she said something afterward about going in a machine, but what she meant by that I don't know because though I couldn't see who was driving, it was a pony cart she went off in and no mistake."

He stared at her thunderstruck and then said, "Davis X. McKenna. *Deus ex machina.*" He gave a great shout of laughter. "Lucy, you're a wonder. If you lose your job, apply to me by way of Lady Harewood and I'll see that you find another place." A gold coin found its way into her hand from his, and then he was gone.

At Harewood Hall Jessica was in the yellow sitting room with Lady Harewood, apologetically recounting the day's adventure. The high-spirited twins had been sent off to the kitchen by their mother to beg some sandwiches from Cook, as she was a great believer in the calming effect of food on growing boys—or at any rate they couldn't talk so much with their mouths full.

"I am *so* sorry about involving the boys in such a *disreputable* adventure, ma'am," Jessica said. "I never meant for anyone of the family to be troubled, but it was quite my fault for sending that note to the stables. Otherwise they never would have known. The thing was, I wasn't perfectly sure I could get away from Harry by myself and I couldn't think how I would get back to Harewood. I expect it was the blow on the head that addled me so that I couldn't think more sensibly."

"Well, you weren't thinking clearly, I'll grant you," Lady Harewood agreed. "You should have sent for Harewood himself, who would have taken the greatest pleasure in dealing with that scoundrel. On the other hand, that would have cheated the twins out of a really splendid adventure. Imagine, being able at the age of thirteen to ride *ventre à terre* to rescue a maiden in distress! They're in transports of delight, and I shouldn't wonder if they'll be a bit above themselves for days on end."

"But I am so humiliated at being involved in such shabby goings-on," Jessica said bitterly. "I can't think what aberration overcame Harry. Not that there's much I would put past him, but he doesn't even *like* me. And suddenly out of a clear sky to come and propose marriage!" She shuddered. "And to say it was his father's dying wish—that is patent nonsense. His father never gave me to understand I was good enough to marry anyone, let alone his precious son. And Harry was nowhere in the vicinity when his father died, so to say he is honoring a deathbed wish is absurd—not that Harry would be likely to honor *anything*, beyond a good racehorse perhaps. And even if it had been true, *I* certainly wouldn't feel bound to honor such a wish. No power on earth could make me wed Harry Broyles, even if he'd kept me locked up in that inn for a month. I'd rather be ruined than married to him, and so I told him. I wonder if loose living can have sent him completely around the bend, because unless he's quite insane, I can't think of any explanation for what he did."

At that moment the door burst open and Lord Markham stormed in. He had seen the pony cart in the stable yard and Jemmy had said, "They're back," as the viscount tossed his reins to him, but it seemed quite necessary to him to confront the lady herself without delay.

Somehow, in a way he could not have explained, at the sight of her sitting quite undamaged and conversing calmly with his sister, all the anxiety, tension, and final relief of the past hours seemed to transmute themselves into anger.

"Well," he said scathingly, "I see you have managed to extricate yourself from another scrape."

Both women turned astonished eyes on him.

"Heaven only knows what goes on when I'm not around," he said bitterly, "but every time I appear on the scene, I find you involved in another predicament, and this one is the worst yet."

Jessica went white at the unexpectedness of the attack and stared at him blankly. "I'm sure I don't know what you mean. I will admit my fault in letting Harry abduct me, though how I could have guessed he meant to do such an *outré* thing I'm sure I don't know. I *wish* I hadn't gotten into his curricle, but he is my cousin and it never occurred to me I stood in any actual danger from him. But when you say I am *always* falling into scrapes, you have me quite at a loss."

He opened his mouth, then closed it again and bit his lip as it occurred to him that the other scrapes she had been in were of his own imagining—the assignation in the stables which turned out to be a tutoring session with Jemmy, the falsely reported engagement to the curate, the proposal from the seventy-year-old Duke of Salford which turned out to be a moss-gathering expedition. He could hardly charge her with any of them, but his fury had to have some vent.

"You had no business walking with my nieces along

a public road where a man like Harry Broyles could accost you."

She rose with dignity. "I was not on a public road. I was on Harewood Drive. And now if you will excuse me . . . I have been kidnapped today. I've been knocked unconscious. I've stuffed myself with enough food to feed a family of five for a week. I do not feel well enough to continue this conversation."

Lady Harewood slipped an arm around Jessica's shoulders and gave her a comforting squeeze. "Do go up to your room and lie down, my dear. I'll send Rose up later to see if you fancy a cup of tea or some broth."

When Jessica had gone, her head high, her shoulders stiff with reproach, Eugenia rounded on her brother. "What on earth has gotten into you, Robert, hectoring the poor child like that? I think you've run as mad as Harry Broyles."

His lordship said no word to defend himself, as he was wondering uneasily if his sister's accusation were true.

Jessica was not down to breakfast the next morning. His sister said she had ordered her to keep to her bedchamber until noon, and as the viscount had previously announced his intention of staying only two nights, he realized he would not be able to rectify the impression his unconsidered words had had on the girl. Well, perhaps it was just as well. How could he explain himself to her, after all, when even he did not understand what had made him cut up at her like that. She was a plaguey little chit, no doubt about it, always seeming to bring out the worst in him. He did not wish her ill, but on the whole felt well pleased to remove himself from her vicinity. He did drop a word of advice to his brother-in-law, however, about speaking to the local magistrate regarding Harry Broyles.

After a brief stay at home seeing to the estate and enjoying some quiet talks with his mother, the viscount returned to London again to find that the newest rage of the season was Lady Melissa Nashbourne, a creamy-skinned blonde heiress of eighteen summers.

She was said to have a lively wit in addition to her undeniable beauty. The viscount danced with her once at the Tatlocks', twice at the Millimans' ball, endured the insipidity of the refreshments at Almack's on three occasions in order to waltz with her, as she had been given approval by no less a personage than that most redoubtable of patronesses, Mrs. Drummond Burrell, and he could be found tooling her around Hyde Park in his high-perch phaeton on many a fine morning.

Needless to say, he was not the only aspirant to her favor. Indeed, he was not seen to be quite so particular in his attentions as to cross the line, but her mother was observed to wear a most complacent look when they stepped out onto the floor together.

As Markham was more or less going through the long-practiced motions without giving very much thought to the matter, it was not until several weeks had passed that it occurred to him that Lady Melissa had no opinions, and as for her vaunted lively wit, it seemed to consist for the most part in giggling and dimpling at any and all humorous sallies put forth for her entertainment, and though the dimple was indeed delicious, he could not see that much wit was involved.

One night during a cold collation at White's, Lady Melissa's name was mentioned most admiringly. Ralph Winterbone turned to Lord Markham and said jestingly, "They say that even though her father is a mere baron, he's rich enough to buy an abbey. You'd better make your move quickly, Robert, before she takes it into her head to hold out for a marquis."

The viscount looked at his friend coldly. "And when was the news put about that I'm hanging out for a rich wife?"

"No such thing," Mr. Winterbone soothed, "but money never hurts, does it? Especially when it comes so beautifully packaged."

"It seems to me that if Lady Melissa has so much money, it would make more sense for her to choose a poor man who needs it."

Winterbone laughed. "And for you to choose a poor girl!"

"Why not?" Markham asked. "Surely one of the pleasures of being rich is being able to choose where I wish, and if I should choose some girl to whom my wealth can make a happy difference, then all the better."

There was general laughter around the table, but the viscount did not hear it because a face had risen in his mind's eye eclipsing his surroundings—a waif's face with intelligent gray eyes and a faintly mocking mouth, a face that had intruded more and more often of late into his thoughts.

Suddenly he wished to be away from his friends. Pushing back his chair, he took his leave with mention of a fictitious engagement and began to walk in the cool night air. The sky was clearer than usual; he could see more stars, and it seemed to him he could see other things more clearly as well.

He could see that his halfhearted pursuit of Lady Melissa was a gesture only, stemming from habit rather than desire. He could see why he had become bored with Carolyn Warriner almost at the moment of deciding to offer for her. And most clearly of all, he could see why he had displayed such unseemly wrath when Jessica Windom had found herself in a dangerous escapade. Exasperating she might be, but she was the only girl he knew who had never bored him. Against all odds, in that wretched, loveless home Monty Broyles had provided for her, she had grown up intelligent, warm, resourceful. There was a richness and a variety in her character that made other women seem as flat as a drawing in a fashion magazine.

But would she have him?—that was the question. He had never done anything to endear himself to her, and he was not fool enough to think that his money and position would cause her to fall into his arms. She was made of sterner stuff than these pampered young misses on the Marriage Mart. He thought with chagrin that she might well give him one of those cool looks of hers and turn him down flat.

He would have to work to win her love, but no matter how long it took, he knew he must do it, because somehow it had happened, without his knowing it, that his heart was wholly hers.

He had first to go on a trip to his northern estate in answer to his bailiff's request. Then before going on to Harewood Hall—and Jessica—he would travel down to Ashendene for Christmas, as his mother was expecting him, and apprise her of the astonishing news. He hoped she would be happy for him. Not every mother would welcome a penniless, nameless girl as her son's bride. But his mother had never denied him anything. Surely she would not wish him denied of the one thing which he now perceived as essential to his happiness.

He could hardly wait to begin his journey.

there much longer. I have my way to make in the world."

Chapter Ten

Lady Sarah rapped gently at her husband's study door. When he had bid her enter, she said apologetically, "I'm sorry to trouble you when you're working on your sermon, my love, but there is a boy here from the inn, sent with a message, and he says he was told to wait for an answer. Shall I send him away again?"

He pushed aside the clutter of papers on his writing table. "No, it's quite all right. I was just finishing."

She brought him the note in a stiff envelope sealed with red wax. He spread the single sheet of paper out and began to read, a puzzled frown deepening on his face. "This is odd," he said.

"What is it, love?"

"It seems to be from a lawyer who is looking for a young lady. He says as she is one of my parishioners, he thought I might know where she can be found. But this is the confusing part. He seems to have expected to find her at Gray Gables and was quite at a loss when no one there knew of her. Have they turned off any housemaids from there lately, do you know? I do hope no young woman who worked there is in any sort of trouble."

"Mary Gorman left right after Monty died," his wife said. "At the moment I believe there are only the housekeeper and cook and two maids, but I saw both of the girls in the village last week. What is the missing girl's name?"

"Miss Wyndham," he said and then looked up, startled. "Dear me! I never thought—because it looks quite different; he spells it W-y-n-d-h-a-m, but it sounds like Windom, doesn't it? Do you suppose he can be looking for Jessica?"

"Well, if he doesn't even know how to spell her name, I can't think it would be anything of importance. Perhaps he has been asking around the district for this Miss Wyndham and someone misunderstood and told him there was a Miss Windom at Gray Gables, though I can't think who it might have been, because outside of ourselves, who knew that she used the name Windom?"

"Well, that must be the answer, nevertheless. I suppose I had better see him," he said, pulling a sheet of paper toward him and taking up his quill to pen a note.

"I'll go and tell Cook there will be a guest for tea," Lady Sarah said.

Mr. Alfred Potterby was a rotund, florid-faced gentleman of less than average height who wore an air of deep concern. "It's very good of you to see me, Vicar," he said. "I have been in something of a pucker since my very unsatisfactory call at Gray Gables. I feel as if that housekeeper must be all about in the head, insisting she's never heard of Miss Wyndham. I hope you can help me."

"Perhaps we should clarify," Mr. Raynes said. "Is it by any chance Miss Jessica Windom you're looking for?"

Relief spread over the little man's face. "Yes, of course. Then you *do* know her?"

"We know a Miss Jessica Windom, but her name is spelled W-i-n-d-o-m, so unless you have it wrong, it can't be the same girl."

Now consternation spread over Mr. Potterby's face again. "There can scarcely be two Jessica Wyndhams in this small place," he said. "And it is you who have the spelling wrong. Though no matter how it is spelled, I fail to see why the housekeeper at Gray Gables should deny the existence of the young lady when I know for a fact it has been her home for the past fifteen years."

"I think perhaps I can suggest an explanation," Lady Sarah put in. "Jessica was generally known as Jessie Broyles. It is quite possible the housekeeper is unaware that she called herself Jessica Windom."

"*Called* herself that? Well, why should she not?" he asked. "Her name *is* Jessica Wyndham. However, this seems to clear up the matter of her whereabouts. I shall return to Gray Gables and inquire for Miss Broyles."

"Well, I'm afraid she is no longer living there," the vicar said.

Mr. Potterby set down his teacup with a click. "No longer living there? Why was I not notified? Where is she?"

131

Though Lady Sarah was puzzled as to why Mr. Potterby should have been notified, his demeanor was one of such genuine distress that she said quickly, "Jessica is at the home of the Viscount Markham's sister, Lady Harewood, at Harewood Hall near Wexford."

Relief was apparent in the very posture of the lawyer as he took a muffin, the first food he had allowed himself, and leaned more comfortably back in his chair. "Oh, that's all right, then, if she is paying a visit."

"It's not precisely that," Lady Sarah said. "She has been there since her cousin Monty Broyles died last winter."

Mr. Potterby frowned. "An extended visit, certainly. She must have been a very close friend of Lord Markham's sister."

"They were not previously acquainted," Lady Sarah said. "The viscount's mother arranged it. You see, Jessica has take a position as the Harewoods' governess."

The uneaten half of Mr. Potterby's muffin dropped from his fingers to his plate unregarded. "*Governess! Position!* Surely you are making a jest."

"My wife is not making a jest," the vicar said stiffly. "And I assure you that Jessica is perfectly qualified."

The man looked from one earnest face to the other. "Miss Wyndham has taken a position as governess," he said slowly, as if testing the words. "Is she—is she eccentric, then?"

The vicar bristled. "She is a most sensible young woman. I fail to see any eccentricity in taking up a respectable position in a household such as Harewood

Hall, where she is given, so she assures us, every consideration."

"She could not stay at Gray Gables very comfortably after Mr. Broyles's death," Lady Sarah put in. "You see, the relative who had served as hostess left and Jessica would have been without a chaperone. Besides, she must have gone out into the world eventually."

"But why did she not set up her own household, then?" Mr. Potterby inquired. "She should have applied to us."

Lady Sarah began to wonder if the little man were deranged. "Just what is your relationship to Miss Windom?" she asked.

"Why, my firm handles the legal details of her estate. We should have been notified immediately of Mr. Broyles's demise." He sounded aggrieved. "We learned of it quite by chance, though of course we would have discovered it when Mr. Broyles failed to appear for the yearly accounting in January."

"The accounting?" the vicar said, bewildered.

"Why, yes. Naturally Mr. Broyles had to give an accounting of the expenses incurred in his guardianship before her allowance was paid out for the next year."

"Do you mean to say Monty Broyles received *money* for caring for Jessica?" he asked in surprise.

Now Mr. Potterby was the one to look as if he suspected his host were somewhat wanting for sense. "Of course he received monies as her guardian," he said patiently.

"But where did it come from?"

"Why, from her estate, of course. Had we realized it

was necessary for her to remove from Gray Gables, naturally we would have been willing to increase her allowance, though Mr. Haselipp has always held the line that three thousand pounds per annum was quite enough until she attained her majority. But Mr. Broyles's death does make a difference."

Neither his host nor hostess could find a word to say for some moments and simply sat staring. Finally Lady Sarah shook her head slightly and cleared her throat. "Mr. Potterby, as you say, there can't be two Jessica Windoms in Monty Broyles's care, but nothing you have told us fits the facts as we know them to apply to our Jessica."

"Just what facts do you know, Lady Sarah?"

"Monty Broyles brought home an orphaned girl when she was three years old. She was alone in the world, destitute. He gave her a roof over her head, food to eat, lessons from my husband, and very little else. When he died, she was penniless and went out to work as a governess. Now you come here with a fantastic story about estates and three thousand pounds a year. Nothing makes any sense."

As she had spoken, Mr. Potterby's ruddy face took on an almost purple hue. "I can only believe that your acquaintance with the family must be remote," he said coldly. "Destitute, indeed. When Miss Wyndham's father died, Mr. Broyles was appointed her guardian by her father's wish. His entire estate was left to her and an allowance of three thousand a year has been paid to her guardian in order to provide her with all the elegances of life to which an heiress in her position is entitled. You may feel that three thousand pounds was a niggardly amount, but it hardly makes her destitute or penniless, and in the opinion of her trustees, it was a sum sufficient to her needs. We do not believe in depleting an estate unnecessarily."

"Mr. Potterby," the vicar said, "we are talking at cross purposes. What my wife was trying to tell you is that the girl, Jessica Windom, has not had three thousand a year spent on her upkeep, nor three hundred, nor even thirty."

The man simply stared. "But that is impossible."

"I don't believe she ever had a dress in her life that wasn't handed down from one of the Broyles girls," Lady Sarah said, "until recently, and then she made her own from cloth that was given to her, and a difficult time we had of it, finding ways to get her to accept it. She never had a governess, nor was sent to school, though her education was the finest, thanks to my husband. Nor did she ever have her own horse, or books of her own, or *anything* beyond a mean little room under the eaves and the very indifferent food served at the Gray Gables table. And now you try to tell us she is an heiress. If that is true, where were her trustees that they did not make it their business to find out how things were going on with her?"

She was flushed with indignation and looked so fierce that Mr. Potterby began to sputter.

"We have had a complete accounting each year from her guardian," he said testily, "who was chosen by her own father."

"Well, it begins to look," said the vicar sternly, "as if her guardian was—" he paused and finished with unaccustomed vehemence "—a black-hearted liar."

There was a pregnant silence. Some of the color drained away from Mr. Potterby's rosy cheeks. "If you were not a man of the cloth," he said at last, sounding dazed, "I should have to disbelieve you. I can scarcely imagine even now that such a fraud has been perpetrated. Mr. Broyles has turned over to us such an exact accounting of how the money was spent: so much for clothing, for her horses, for her private groom, her maid, the perch phaeton he purchased for her last year—"

Lady Sarah gave a most undignified snort. "Her maid! Her groom! If she has ever *ridden* in a perch phaeton it is more than I know, and the only riding she has done was secretly when the stable boy took pity on her."

"We have had yearly letters from her governess reporting on her progress," he said. "We have not been remiss in seeing that our client's needs were met. No one could accuse us of such a thing. Why, Mr. Haselipp was very willing to advance an extra sum to purchase the phaeton when Mr. Broyles told us what an excellent whip she was and how she had her heart set on it, as well as an amount to cover the expenses of the ball in her honor last spring. I cannot believe—"

"If you cannot *believe*, Mr. Potterby," Lady Sarah cried, "then I suggest you call on the local gentry and ask how many of them were invited to this ball. Ask which of them has seen her driving her perch phaeton. Try to find a trace of this governess who wrote such convincing reports."

"But where has the money gone?" he inquired with a rather pathetic plea.

"I should rather guess the greater share went into Monty Broyles's stables," the vicar said grimly. "Horses were his passion. He was always on the point of finding the racehorse that would make his fortune. His enthusiasm for racing outstripped his judgment, however. He also disappeared to London for some months each year, where I make no doubt he lived expensively."

"And some of the money went on the backs of his daughters, I should guess," Lady Sarah said indignantly. "And to pay for their come-outs and to provide dowries, for how else such fusby-faced, mean-dispositioned girls ever found husbands would be a mystery."

"The mystery is," her husband put in, "how Broyles ever got hold of Jessica to begin with."

"I can tell you that. It was all quite aboveboard and legal." The little man seemed eager to show that his firm was above reproach *there*. "Miss Wyndham's parents, Jack Wyndham and his wife, had been living abroad for some years. We were his legal firm. When the child was three years old, her mother died during an influenza epidemic in Vienna. Her father, knowing himself to be fatally ill as well, appealed to his wife's cousin, who happened to be in Vienna at the time, to bring his daughter back to England and care for her. He arrived in London with the child and an Austrian nurse. He had documents to prove her birth and a letter from her father introducing Mr. Broyles and stating that he was a cousin to whose care he had entrusted his daughter. The papers were all quite authentic. They were witnessed by a member of the

Austrian embassy who was a friend of Wyndham's. When the legal matters had been arranged with regard to Mr. Broyles's guardianship, he took the child down to Gray Gables."

"Did you never search for closer relations—grandparents, perhaps?"

Mr. Potterby bridled. "You seem quick to accuse, Mr. Raynes, but I assure you that our firm did not shirk its duties. We had long handled Mr. Wyndham's affairs. There was no need to search for grandparents because we knew they were dead. The only relative Mr. Wyndham had left was a sister in Scotland, but he had broken with his family years before, and it was clear from his letter that he was giving his daughter into Monty Broyles's care, so searching for relatives would have been quite inappropriate. Broyles was appointed guardian by her own father's wish."

A thoughtful silence fell upon the party. At last Mr. Raynes said, "And what is to happen now?"

"That is why I came to Gray Gables. Having learned of Mr. Broyles's demise, we knew that a new guardian must be appointed. Under ordinary circumstances it would be her cousin, Mr. Harry Broyles—"

"No!" Lady Sarah cried in alarm.

"—but of course that seems unlikely now. I shall have to check out your story, of course," he said with dignity. "Though you are the vicar—even if you were archbishop—I shall have to make thorough inquiries as to whether the young woman residing at Harewood Hall is indeed Miss Jessica Wyndham. And if it is so, why, then she must be apprised of the situation."

Lady Sarah looked at her husband. "Even happy news, if it is of such great moment, can be a shock. And of course the news cannot be all happiness to her, knowing she has been cheated all these years...." There was a question in her face.

"Yes, my dear. I quite agree. I think it would be in order if you were to pay a visit to Harewood Hall."

Chapter Eleven

A more high-strung young lady might have been expected to swoon away and tumble off the little gilt-legged chair in the Yellow Saloon. Jessica merely clasped her hands very tightly in her lap, her face turning so pale that her enormous gray eyes deepened almost to black.

"I don't believe I understand you, sir."

Lady Sarah, simply but charmingly dressed in a plum-colored traveling dress and seated beside Lady Harewood on a striped French sofa, thought that it was little wonder the poor child didn't understand Mr. Potterby's circumlocutions and decided it was time to lay the truth out plain as mutton. "It's quite simple, love," she said. "Your father left his fortune to you, and that rogue Monty Broyles kept you in ignorance of it and appropriated the money for himself."

"Ah-uh," Mr. Potterby cleared his throat. "A suit could of course be brought against the Broyles heirs, but a preliminary investigation leads me to believe that precious little would be realized above the sale of the horses. And as far as the culpability of our firm—"

Jessica waved her hand as one would at a bother-

141

some gnat and said, "No, no; that doesn't matter. But my father truly did leave me an inheritance?"

"His entire fortune," Mr. Potterby asserted.

Color came into Jessica's cheeks then and she put one hand to her eyes just for a moment. "It doesn't matter then that Monty wasted it all. Just knowing that he meant for me to have it—" Her voice broke slightly.

"Wasted it all!" Mr. Potterby said sharply. "How can you think that Haselipp, Potterby and Haselipp would allow such a thing?"

Lady Sarah coughed and turned an ironic gaze upon him, but he stared her down. "It is true we have been gravely misled by what I can only term Mr. Broyles's *villainy*, but he has not wasted your fortune, only the allowance made to you for the past fifteen years."

"Which seems to me quite outrageous enough," Lady Harewood put in indignantly.

He cast her an anguished glance. "However, you may be assured that the bulk of your inheritance is quite intact."

Jessica's eyes had been lowered during this exchange, but now she looked up rather embarrassed and said, "But will it not be contested, then?"

"Contested? By whom?"

"By—by—did my father leave no *legitimate* heirs?"

The lawyer's face purpled. "Legitimate? You are his legitimate—and only—heir."

Now Jessica did sway slightly in her chair but quickly recovered herself. She leaned forward. "Oh, sir, pray do not trifle with me. Is it truly so? My parents were married?"

"Where could you get such a distempered notion? Of course they were married. Oh, to be sure, it was against their family's wishes—that's why they went to live on the Continent—but there was nothing havey-cavey about the marriage."

Tears welled in Jessica's eyes and her mouth trembled. Lady Sarah was out of her seat in an instant and on her knees beside the slight little form, a hand on the dark curls pulling Jessica's head to her shoulder.

She clung there trembling just for an instant, then pulled herself upright again and, looking into her friend's loving face, said, "To have been told all these years that I was a 'base-born brat' only kept out of the workhouse by Monty's charity! If he weren't dead, I should—I should kill him!"

Lady Sarah laughed. "You would not have the chance, because I would have done it myself as soon as I heard Mr. Potterby's story."

"Ohh," Jessica's eyes widened as a thought occurred to her. "The money! Now I understand why that loathsome Harry wanted to marry me. He must have known about my inheritance!"

"Why, of course. It's plain as a pikestaff," Lady Harewood said.

"To marry you?" Lady Sarah was startled.

"I didn't write you of it because it was so disagreeable, but he came to see me with some round tale of its being his father's deathbed wish that we wed. Have you ever heard such a plumper?"

"Well, I suppose Monty did mean to marry you off to Harry to keep the money in the family, only while Monty was alive and you hadn't attained your majority, there was no hurry about it."

"But Harry must have been afraid you'd hear from the lawyers after his father died," Lady Harewood said with an excited gleam, "and that was why he kidnapped you."

Both Lady Sarah and Mr. Potterby were struck dumb by this revelation and insisted on hearing the whole story.

"Of course if he *had* been able to intimidate you, once the knot was legally tied, he'd have had control of your fortune," Mr. Potterby said. "He must have been counting upon getting the deed done before the allowance was to be paid in January, at which time our firm would certainly have been made aware of his father's demise."

"Harry is as bad as Monty," Lady Sarah said with a shudder. "Like father, like son."

"*Kakoú kórakos kakón oón,*" Jessica murmured. "From a bad crow a bad egg."

"Well, they are both villains," Lady Harewood exclaimed. "What I can't understand is why Mr. Wyndham should have delivered Jessica into the hands of such a man."

There was a puzzled silence at that, and then Mr. Potterby said, "I can't suppose he was closely acquainted with Mr. Broyles, who was merely a third or fourth cousin of his wife's. But by chance Broyles happened to be in Vienna when Mrs. Wyndham died, and he knew himself to be on the point of expiring. It must have seemed to him a reasonable thing to do—to send her back to England with virtually the only relative she had." He frowned. "Mr. Wyndham did have a sister, but we assumed the breach between him and his family was too deep. They disowned him when he married, though in the end he did inherit half of his father's money. Well, it is a very long story and I am not perfectly conversant with all the details. Perhaps some friend of your father's may be found who could enlighten you further."

"Oh, my," Jessica cried, suddenly struck. "If it is really true that I have some money of my own—"

They all looked at her expectantly. "—Why, then I can send Jemmy Dawson to school myself. Only I must start in at once to improve his grammar, because despite his quick mind, it is really quite atrocious."

Lady Sarah's lips curved as she gazed with affection at her protégée. How like Jessica, how very like her when offered a whole new life, that the first change in circumstance she thought of was that now she could educate the poor stable boy she had written about to her friends with such enthusiasm. And she wondered if it had struck the others as it had her—not once had Jessica inquired as to the extent of her fortune.

When Jessica went up to her pretty little yellow and white bedchamber that night, her head was drooping with the fatigue caused by the emotional impact of Mr. Potterby's revelations. Lady Sarah had noted the slightly glazed look in her eyes and insisted she retire. "We'll have plenty of time to talk it all over at length, my love, as Lady Harewood has very kindly invited me to stay as long as I like."

Jessica had kissed her friend, pressed her employer's hand gratefully, and bid Mr. Potterby good-bye, as he had insisted on putting up at a nearby inn and planned to make an early start to London the next day.

But once tucked up into her bed, Jessica's thoughts would not stop spinning. Everything was so new and a little frightening as well, but she clung with a fierce thrill of happiness to the thought that she had had parents who loved her. "A young lady of consequence," Mr. Potterby had solemnly called her. Her lips curved sleepily. It was a preposterous notion. She was the same Jessica Windom as she had always been, no matter how her name was spelled. And yet—and yet— the notion did just cross her mind that as Miss Wyndham, with an independence, there were certain options open to her that might well have remained closed to Miss Windom the governess, with the name she had no right to. Perhaps even marriage.

She shivered a little under the warm eiderdown, but from what cause she could not have said.

Neither Lady Sarah nor Lady Harewood arose early the next morning, but they met in the breakfast parlor, rather glad that Jessica was not downstairs yet, as they had many plans to discuss with regard to her future, some few of which they were in accord could best be done in her absence.

"You were always a good girl, Eugenia," Lady Sarah commented. "And now you're being a perfect trump about this. Not every woman would be so happy to have her governess snatched away."

"It will be a wrench to see her go," Lady Harewood admitted, "but no one could be so cruel as to not be happy for her. And I've known she wouldn't stay forever. Sooner or later some man would have come along with the imagination to see past those governessy clothes of hers to the real Jessica." She paused. "She may not *take* in London, you know."

"She can be too outspoken, I know. And I'm afraid she is something of a bluestocking. Still, you never know. I wish I had the dressing of her."

They went on to speak of all sorts of agreeable plans concerning clothes, houses, introductions. "The countess Lieven is a particular friend of mine," Lady Harewood commented, and needed to say no more for Lady Sarah instantly to understand the importance of the statement, since one of the prime requisites for a young woman on the point of making her entrance on the social scene was a voucher from the patronesses of Almack's, which would admit her to its rather stuffy but almost hallowed portals. A young lady not allowed to attend the Almack's balls might as well be buried in the country teaching the alphabet to children.

When at last they had settled so many points between them that they were ready to lay a plan of action before Jessica, Lady Harewood summoned Rose to go and awaken her.

"Why, ma'am, she breakfasted hours ago and has been in the schoolroom with the young ladies ever since."

The two women shook their heads, and Lady Sarah said, "It may not be so easy as we had hoped."

"At any rate there are two of us to bully her," Lady Harewood said kindly. "In numbers there is strength."

When at last Jessica arrived in the morning room where she had been directed, rather flushed from hurrying, she had a half-worried look as if it would not surprise her so very much to hear that the astonishing news of last night had all been a mistake.

"Well, my dear, you were at your duties early, I hear," Lady Harewood said. "Have you told the girls of your good fortune?"

Jessica smiled. "Yes, I have, and they were quite set up about it. Claire vowed she was the only one among her acquaintance to have an heiress for a governess."

The two older ladies exchanged glances. "As I cannot stay *very* long away from home, my love, I think perhaps we had best begin helping you make your plans," Lady Sarah said.

"What do you mean?" Jessica asked, puzzled.

"Well, have you had time yet to decide on any course of action you want to take in view of Mr. Potterby's disclosure?"

"Why, yes, I mentioned about the schooling for Jemmy. And I am hoping that Mr. Potterby can indeed find someone who once knew my father well enough to tell me his history and that of my mother. He promised to try."

"That is fine, Jessica, but we were thinking more along the lines of where and how you plan to live."

Jessica blinked uncertainly. "Why, must I leave here, ma'am?"

"My dear child, you make it sound as if I am turning you off without a reference. Of course it is no such thing. But you will want to set up your own establishment. You can hardly mean to continue working for your bread."

"It would put Eugenia in the oddest possible position, you know," Lady Sarah said gravely, "if it were to be known that her governess is so very rich."

Jessica gasped. "Oh, surely not nearly so rich as all that; but I do see what you mean. I hadn't thought of it that way. But may I stay until after Christmas? The girls and I had so many plans for entertainments."

"That would be very generous of you. And it would give me time to search for a replacement and give the girls time to accustom themselves to your leaving. Not that you could possibly *be* replaced, but we'll have to find someone to teach the girls."

Jessica's brow wrinkled in thought. "Perhaps I could buy that empty cottage near the vicarage and fix it up," she said at last. "I think it would be quite pretty if the shutters were mended and some new steps built. Do you think that would serve?"

"No," Lady Sarah said bluntly. "It wouldn't serve at all. I think you should hire a house in London."

Jessica looked rather staggered at the suggestion.

"Just think of all the educational opportunities you would enjoy. The British Museum. The Royal Academy. The theaters. The opera. Lectures. Exhibitions. What a dismal waste to bury yourself in the country without first having tasted what the world has to offer in the way of intellectual stimulation."

Jessica considered. "Yes. I always did dream that

someday I would see London, but it is such a new notion that I can simply—do as I please."

"But a very agreeable one, surely," Lady Sarah said, relieved that the first hurdle was past. "Now of course you will need some respectable woman to live with you, and if you have no firm ideas to the contrary, I wondered if you would like to consider my cousin Tessa, Lady Wellby. Do you remember meeting her when she visited the vicarage once?"

"Yes, indeed, and I liked her very well, but why should you suppose she would wish to come and live with me?"

"I'm sure she would like it of all things," Lady Sarah said confidently. "Since her husband died three years ago, she has been residing in Surrey with her son, and I fear she is nearly moped to death. Her daughter-in-law is the kindest girl alive but *will* cosset Tessa, which she detests. They are a rather serious-minded couple, and the challenge of launching a girl into London society is the very thing Tessa needs to give her a new interest in life. If you will have her, that is."

Jessica had shrunk back in alarm at the words "launch a girl into London society." Now she said, "But you can't suppose, ma'am, that I mean to try to enter *that* set. Even though I now know that my birth was respectable, I have no acquaintance among society."

"You are acquainted with my brother Robert," Lady Harewood said.

"I—I think L-lord Markham would not be pleased to introduce me into his set," Jessica stammered.

"If you are teasing yourself over that ridiculous scene he made after Harry Broyles had carried you off, don't. Who knows what maggot he had taken into his head. He was very likely just in bad frame that day. And of course I was not suggesting that a gentleman introduce you into society, but only that in him you do have at least one acquaintance in London."

"At any rate that is not important, for introducing you is just what my cousin Tessa can do and will like doing. And if you try to say that you would not be able to go on comfortably in society, you will make me very angry, for were you not my pupil as well as my husband's for many years, Jessica?"

"Yes, but—"

"We are not suggesting you make particular friends of the dandy set, but while the theaters and museums are open to all, unless you are invited to dinner parties and soirées, you won't meet any of the interesting people whose company you might enjoy."

"Yes, I see what you mean," Jessica said thoughtfully. "Well, I can only be very grateful if your cousin would indeed take me under her wing."

"It's settled then," Lady Harewood said briskly. "Why don't you run on back to the schoolroom, then, my dear, if you are indeed willing to continue with the girls' lessons for just a little longer."

When she had left the room, two pairs of eyes met in silent communication. Then Lady Sarah breathed a sigh of relief. "It's always best to get over heavy ground quickly, I believe."

"I think she will adjust to her situation," Lady Harewood said. "There's nothing like a becoming new bon-

151

net to give one confidence. And when she first sees herself in a really becoming ball gown, she'll realize she is not out of place in society. I only hope she may *take*."

Chapter Twelve

The Viscount Markham arrived at Ashendene in time to support his mother through the felicity of enjoying Christmas visits from his younger sister Maxine, her husband, and their hopeful brood of three, plus his mother's Aunt Lavinia with her widowed son, and two spinster cousins of the late viscount.

As Aunt Lavinia and the spinster cousins fell into a violent disagreement over the relative merits of pug dogs and setters, an argument which was fought and refought until past New Year's, and Lavinia's son displayed his innate contempt for children as well as a decided predilection for port, and since Maxine took utmost care that her offspring were introduced into every possible and some nearly impossible entertainments, it could not be said that it was a relaxing holiday. However, as his mother enjoyed nothing so much as having her grandchildren about her, and as she had great skill at smoothing ruffled feathers and turning a deaf ear to spiteful insinuations, the viscount bore it all with a fair degree of patience and lived in anticipation of the moment when they would all be off and he could have a peaceful moment alone with his mother in which to discuss the matter that was ever paramount in his mind.

As the days wore on, his patience wore a little thinner, but contrary to his exasperated expectations the visits did eventually come to an end. He joined his mother in the library after dinner that evening and sank into a chair by the fire with relief, stretching one leg out to rest a foot negligently on the fender.

"Isn't it pleasant to have a moment to ourselves, Robert? I've scarcely had a chance to talk to you."

"Indeed it is pleasant, Mama."

"I was just thinking, I believe I shall get a pug."

He grinned. "Doing it much too brown, Mama. Though it would serve you right if I rode over to Hartlethorpe and brought one home tomorrow. Dinworthy raises them, you know, and has foisted them onto half the neighborhood."

"Speaking of that, I haven't even had an opportunity to tell you our biggest neighborhood on-dit. Have you heard about Jessica Windom?"

His pulse quickened and he looked at her quickly, but at once began to breathe calmly again. He had heard all sorts of stories about Jessica and jumped each time to the wrong conclusion, but that was before he knew his own heart. Nothing his mother could tell him would make a happ'orth of difference. She was his love, and nothing, *nothing* he heard of her could change his resolution to win her for his own.

"No, Mama, I haven't heard anything about her since I last visited Eugenia," he said steadily.

"It's quite the most fantastic story," his mother said. "It seems she is an heiress!"

"A what?"

"An heiress. And her name isn't Windom. At least it is, but it's spelled *W-y-n-d-h-a-m*. Her father was Jack Wyndham. I believe I was slightly acquainted with his older sister, who went off to live in Scotland and became some sort of recluse. Well, not exactly, but she and the laird she married never show their faces in London. She was not very tonnish. Preferred horses to people, as I recall."

"Yes, yes, Mama," he said impatiently. "But what has that to do with Jessica? With Miss Windom."

"Nothing really, only there was some sort of dust-up when Jack married. The girl was perfectly respectable, but had no fortune."

"Married! Oh, I am so happy for her," he said warmly.

His mother looked at him in surprise.

"That swine of a cousin of hers gave her to understand that her birth was not legitimate. It cut her on the raw, I believe."

Lady Markham's eyes flashed angrily. "I never heard that tale. And what a dastardly lie, because they were married and they went off to Vienna. And later when Jessica was three, they both died of influenza. Monty Broyles was some sort of connection of Jack's wife, and he happened to be in Vienna at the time. On the look for horseflesh, I make no doubt. When he realized he was dying, Jack gave his daughter into Monty's keeping, and he brought her home and became her guardian. The shocking thing is that he received a whacking sum every year for her upkeep—from her father's estate. And we know the poor little thing never saw a penny of it."

"I'm damned!" the viscount said softly.

"Can you imagine, that poor child treated no better than a servant, when all the time it was her money buying clothes for those odious girls and those wild months Monty spent racketing around London, to say nothing of his racehorses. And he never even had the wit to breed winners."

"I don't see how such a thing could have come about."

"Neither do I, but Jack's family had died off before then, except for the sister in Scotland, and Jack's wife had been in the care of an uncle who was dead, too. So I suppose no one in England even knew about the child. And there was Monty with a letter from her father giving him the care of her. There was really no one left to ascertain that she was being well cared for. Lady Sarah thinks that the attorneys who held the money in trust should have looked into her upbringing more carefully, but she says they claim they had no reason for suspicion. Monty presented them with a complete—though false—accounting every year, even letters from her governess, if you please, recounting her progress. Her governess!"

"It's too bad he can't be brought to book for it," the viscount said grimly.

"Yes, except that it's only because of his death that the situation came to light. If he had lived, he would have married her off to Harry before she came into the whole of her inheritance at the age of twenty-one."

"I doubt *that*. She would never have married that great lout," he said angrily.

"Perhaps not, but I'm sure that was Monty's intention. After all, he never let her meet anyone else. And who knows what pressures would have been brought to bear on a friendless girl."

"She wasn't friendless," he objected.

"Except for the Rayneses, she very nearly was. And Sarah says the girl took very good care not to let any of the Broyles household see how close she was to the vicarage. She seemed to sense that they wouldn't allow her to continue to visit them and take lessons if they had known there was any real affection or intimacy involved."

"That must have been why Harry kidnapped her," he said suddenly. "Did you know about that?"

"Yes, Lady Sarah told me. When he came home and found his father dead, he must have known he had to move quickly to get the girl riveted to him or the money would slip out of his grasp. And I'm sure he's lived in expectation of it for years. He's a graceless enough young dog—and not an ounce of goodness in him. Where else would he find an heiress to marry?"

"He belongs in prison," the viscount muttered.

"True, but Jessica won't bring charges, of course. It would be a nine-day wonder. Well, she's had her first brush with a fortune hunter, but I daresay it won't be her last."

"What do you mean?"

"Why, they'll be around her like flies to honey. I don't know the exact amount, but her inheritance is large enough to attract every basket scrambler in London."

"London!" He was startled. "What is she doing in London?"

"She is not there yet, but where else would she go? She can hardly stay on teaching Delphie her letters now. And she would scarcely return to Gray Gables. A widowed cousin of Lady Sarah's is going to take her in hand. Introduce her to the ton. She is a Lady Tessa Wellby, and I only hope she's up to snuff on all counts, because Jessica will need a fierce protectress. When word of her fortune gets around—and it will despite any attempts to keep it quiet—every rattle in town who needs to feather his nest will be making up to her."

"Surely not only those, Mama," he said in some dismay. "Surely some man who sees her true worth and doesn't care for her fortune will be able to teach her to care for him."

"I hope so; but I should think she would have suspicions of anyone who proposes matrimony. She is only a green girl after all, for all her erudition, and the one man who has ever wanted her was Harry—and she knows what attracted him. It's too bad some worthy man didn't chance to see her while she was with Eugenia and still a nobody. A man who had made a push to secure her affection *then* she must have trusted to care for herself alone. . . .

"Well, it grows late, Robert. I shall retire."

He rose and kissed her, and she went up to bed all unknowing of the dagger she had placed in her beloved son's heart.

He had been so sure that nothing she told him could dissuade his intention to win Jessica's love. But she had given him a leveler indeed, for how could he go to Jessica now and tell her that he had fallen deeply in love with her when he believed her to be penniless—that his dearest hope had been to make her his wife? How could he ask her to believe that her fortune, her respectable birth, mattered not at all to him when he had not told her of his love before he learned of the change in her circumstance? She might acquit him of designs on her money; she knew he had no need of it. But how could she ever believe that her namelessness had not mattered to him?

Why had he been such a fool that he had not recognized his feelings earlier? Why had he not posted directly to her as soon as he knew his own heart? If he had gone to Harewood Hall then instead of to his northern estate, would he have been in time?

He poured himself a glass of brandy as a blackness of soul took possession of him. He stared into the fire, his fine-featured face filled with despair. There was no comfort for him anywhere, except that he could be happy for her peace of mind in knowing she had not been abandoned by her father. But as for the money, he considered it a curse. He could have provided for her every need—if only he hadn't been blind so long, been so long a fool.

Chapter Thirteen

The Lady Tessa Wellby swept upon Jessica with all the force of a sudden spring thaw, and though the weather was still frigid, Jessica felt as if an ice jam had suddenly broken up and she was being carried swiftly downstream willy-nilly.

Lady Wellby was tall, spare, and energetic. Jessica could easily see why she would have chafed at living with a daughter-in-law who tried to keep her wrapped in a shawl. Her face, though leaner and lacking the gentle sweetness of her cousin's, did remind Jessica somewhat of Lady Sarah. She dressed herself in simple elegance and had decided opinions on every subject, though she was quite ready, even eager, for Jessica to make decisions for herself—except when it came to how to spend their time.

"You will have plenty of time for seeing the sights when we remove to your house in the spring. Now we must set wheels in motion or it won't be ready for us when the season commences."

Jessica had not dreamed there would be so many decisions. Lady Wellby's well-sprung carriage had carried them, along with an abigail and two postillions, to London, where they moved into a set of rooms at the Pulteney Hotel. Then began the series of interviews with house agents, the inspection of likely sounding dwellings, and when at last one in Portman Place had been settled upon, Lady Wellby had commanded her to decide which of the furniture should be retained and which relegated to the lumber room.

"These draperies will have to go, I think, do you not, my dear?" she asked. "I don't care if this house does belong to a marchioness, they are amazingly horrid with that great lozenge design and that vulgar fringe. I wonder where she can ever have found a draper with such a pattern in his stocks."

"I quite agree," Jessica said. "And now if you will come and look at the Egyptian Salon. It does seem to me a bit *more* Egyptian than I can quite like. The color scheme of terra cotta and citron and black is quite attractive, and I do not object to the lotus columns or the alabaster obelisk, but I think that truncated pyramid with the sphinx on top is really *outré*, don't you?"

Lady Wellby did.

Their plan was to place orders for all the changes that would be required in the house, to decide upon some sort of conveyance for Jessica, and to choose such wardrobe as she would need. Then she would return to Harewood Hall and Lady Wellby to her son's home until all was in readiness.

It had not proved to be quite such a wrenching parting from Claire and Delphie as it might have been, since she knew she would be returning to them for another month or more. Lady Harewood had promised to bring them to London late in the season also, and they had been busily planning excursions they would undertake in Jessica's company.

Mr. Potterby had been most helpful about setting forth a series of figures which he considered a reasonable amount for her to draw for her various expenses. At first she was quite staggered by the very idea of having such sums at her disposal, as she still had the sensation of being a sleeper who might at any moment awaken from a pleasant dream. However, with Lady Wellby's encouragement, she began to overcome her scruples and express her opinions and order new furnishings as if it were the merest commonplace.

She decided the Blue Saloon was enough to give anyone a fit of the dismals and ordered it rehung with red Chinese paper. The only furniture she retained in it were a marble side table and a pair of charming rococo chairs made by Vile and Cobb some forty years earlier and decorated with a delicate design of laurel leaves. For the rest, Lady Wellby had declared it the falsest of economies to reupholster furniture that didn't belong to one, especially since most of it was sadly outmoded, and so Jessica ordered comfortable new stuffed couches and chairs, and of course draperies to replace the gloomy blue ones.

After this signal extravagance she vowed she would be satisfied with the rest of the house as it stood and purchase nothing more, except that at Ince and Mayhew's she could not resist a delightful little writing cabinet nor a set of cane-back chairs for the breakfast parlor to replace the wretchedly uncomfortable ones that were so ornately carved they would bruise one's spine should one be so unwise as to try to lean back.

However, she determined to be pleased with all the pictures and ornaments just as she found them in the house and not spend one guinea in such a frivolous way, and she stuck to this resolve save that she caught sight of a jasperware urn in the most delightful shade of pale green and ornamented in white overlay with figures of the nine muses, and before she knew what she was about, she had purchased it.

At this point she discovered she was a little frightened by her own extravagance—she who had never had two sixpences to rub together. She must be all about in her head to have spent so much. She should have kept the breakfast chairs and been content ever to sit bolt upright, even though the cane-back ones had just come back into fashion and were all the crack. Somehow she could not regret the jasperware urn, however. It was the first beautiful thing she had ever owned.

She decided she would economize on her wardrobe, and she quite rejected the notion of purchasing a carriage. In the latter resolve she was overruled by Lady Wellby, who pronounced it the greatest piece of folly imaginable to think of jaunting about London in a job-carriage.

"Now, my child, I've borne with your crotchets about spending money with greatest patience," she said, to Jessica's surprise, for she felt she had been free-handed to the point of profligacy, "but take my word for it, a carriage is a necessity. We will ask my friend General Gormsley to help us choose one, as he is most knowledgeable in such matters. I do not wish to apply to one of my children's friends in the younger set, as I don't think it will be well for you to be seen until your appearance is a little smarter. First impressions are so important. Unless you would wish to consult with Lady Harewood's brother. He has already seen you at your worst, so there could be no harm in that."

Jessica was conscious of a very odd conflict of emotions at this suggestion. On the one hand it would be very pleasant to see Lord Markham and receive his advice on the purchase of a carriage. On the other hand she thought it probable that he would know from his sister that she was in town and putting up at the Pulteney Hotel, and yet he had not so much as left his card. Of course he might not even be in London at this time, but if he were—Lady Wellby's remarks about not letting herself be seen until she was looking a little smarter struck a sensitive place in her mind, and the assurance that it would not matter about the viscount because he had seen her at her worst somehow failed to make her comfortable.

"I think I should prefer General Gormsley," she said at length. "The last time I met Lord Markham, we somehow rubbed one another to the point of dagger-drawing. I'm not at all sure he would wish to help me choose a carriage."

Lady Wellby raised her eyebrows at this intelligence and attempted to search Jessica's face, but at that moment the young lady had suddenly found it necessary to busy herself with folding her handkerchief into pleats, so only the top of her curls were to be seen.

* * *

General Gormsley's advice was the soundest, and Jessica had soon placed an order for a carriage with brushed-brass hardware and luxurious blue velvet squabs. "We'll wait on the horses until you return to take up residence," he said. "No use to have them eating off you and a groom kicking his heels in idleness while you are out of the city. I presume you'll want a mount as well."

"Oh, yes," Jessica said, "and I should like a horse with spirit. I believe my *style* is not of the first degree of elegance, but I can manage a sweet stepper with no difficulty."

"Well, I'll keep my ears open," the general promised. "One thing—when you get back to town, if you run across Sir Digby Saulsbourne, don't let him talk horses to you. He's a personable fellow, but I never knew him when he wasn't trying to unload a horse or a pair, and take my word for it, you don't want any of his breakdowns. At best they'll be too short in the neck; at worst they'll fall lame within a month."

"I'll remember," Jessica promised, laughing.

Between them Mr. Potterby and Lady Wellby produced five prospective butlers for Jessica to interview. One was entirely too forbidding; one had so high an opinion of his own consequence that he quite put Jessica off him. From among the other three she chose the one with the most intelligent eyes. His name was Burdock, and he undertook to assure her that by the time she returned he would have assembled a staff for her.

She was somewhat taken aback when he asked what color livery her footmen were to be garbed in, but sternly repressed her impulse to fall into a fit of the giggles which would have sunk her quite beneath reproach in his eyes. She managed to answer with some show of confidence that her footmen wore bottle green with no ornamentation.

The most critical part of their shopping, from Lady Wellby's viewpoint, concerned Jessica's wardrobe. "You are not planning to be nip-farthing about your apparel, I trust," she said sternly when Jessica demurred at visiting Madame Therese's establishment in Curzon Street and suggested that a more moderately priced *modiste* might serve equally well. "Let me tell you that for all your intelligence, you are not up to snuff yet, my child, if you think that to patronize a shop where nobody but the shabby-genteels go is a reasonable economy."

At this stricture Jessica subsided meekly. Indeed, after half an hour or so at Madame Therese's she began to enter into the spirit of the thing. "The young lady is so petite that she will of course wish to avoid the three-quarter robe," Madame Therese pronounced. "However, the high-waisted dresses should become her to perfection. And these clinging styles will show off her neat figure to great advantage."

"But not so clinging as to be immodest," Jessica said with a rather worried look.

Madame Therese seemed inclined to take umbrage and drew herself up haughtily. "In this establishment we do not dress young ladies of eighteen *immodestly*."

Just then Lady Wellby exclaimed over a length of delightful coral pink crepe and the moment passed.

When French muslins, cambrics, silks, and spider

gauzes in a rainbow of colors had all been produced for inspection, Madame Therese said firmly, "Only the simplest lines will do—no flounces or heavy ornamentation. We wish to emphasize the perfection of the figure and to create an illusion of height. And I think that we may use unusual colors with a free hand, as the young lady's coloring is adaptable to hues that are something beyond the ordinary."

To this end they decided upon a walking dress in cherry red, a jonquil morning dress, a deep green shot-silk pelisse trimmed with swansdown, and for a ball gown Jessica fell in love with a delicious shade of yellow green the color of new willow leaves. Her riding habit was to be a rich, dark brown velvet which almost exactly matched her curls, and Madame Therese suggested an orange ostrich plume to trim the hat.

The whole of the afternoon passed away, ending with Jessica in a daze after saying yes or no to so many lengths of sprig muslin and jaconets that to save herself she later could not have told how many gowns she had actually settled upon. She clutched at Lady Wellby's arm when they at last reached the street and vowed that she felt quite faint.

Her mentor gave a low laugh. "As well, then, that it is too late to visit the milliner's today."

"Oh, my," Jessica gasped. "I do not think I shall ever become accustomed to not being poor."

"If I have anything to say to it, you will," Lady Wellby said. "Just consider that you are making up for many years of unfair deprivation. I'm sure a less modest girl would be running quite wild, whereas I have to push you to make you spend a farthing."

"A farthing!" she said faintly. "Indeed I shall be afraid to see the reckoning."

"Then we shall have it sent straightway to Mr. Potterby. Do not forget, he has authorized these expenditures, and I make no doubt they are putting no strain on your estate, for Haselipp, Potterby and Haselipp are a great deal too conservative to allow you to do that."

Mlle. Dupuis, the milliner, was able to produce a number of creations which became Jessica's face to a shade. The poke bonnet with the ruffled lemon silk inside the brim was much too pretty not to buy, as was the satin-straw gypsy hat with rose red ribbons that tied beneath the chin. And when it came to the bonnet with the ostrich plumes that completely framed her face in such a piquant manner, there was no doubt whatsoever that it was a confection.

After that there were only slippers to purchase— satin for evening, morocco kid for day, and halfboots; then gloves of York tan, kid, and Limerick gloves for evening; plus a cashmere shawl and one of Norwich silk, two gauze scarfs, and several bandeaus for her hair, which an excellent coiffeuse had cut and arranged for her à la Titus. At last Lady Wellby made the welcome announcement that she believed that, aside from such trifles as reticules and parasols, which might be left until later, their shopping was nearly at an end—unless Jessica would like to purchase some jewelry.

Jessica most definitely would not.

Her reunion with Claire and Delphie was affecting for all three of them. She had brought them presents—a French doll for Delphie and a pagoda-shaped parasol for Claire, as well as silk petticoats for Rose and her sister Lucy.

"Tell us everything you did in London," Claire urged.

"It is the most lowering thing for your preceptress to have to tell you," Jessica said rather crossly, "but I saw remarkably little of the city and nothing at all of the museums and theaters. Lady Wellby would allow me to do nothing but spend money in an attempt to turn me into a grand lady, which indeed I am sure I shall never be. But she has promised that when we go back in the spring, I may see as many sights as I choose, for by then my wardrobe will be ready and I will be fit to be seen. To hear her talk, one would think people go to the Royal Academy not to look at the pictures but to see what other people are wearing. It is the most nonsensical thing! However, she is very kind, and when she was not urging me to purchase more gowns, we had some very interesting conversations. She has traveled widely and once stayed for several months in Venice, and she has such a way of describing things that one almost feels one has been there and seen the gondolas and the Doge's Palace."

"Did you see my brother while you were there?" Lady Harewood wanted to know.

There was an odd little pause, and then Jessica said, rather too brightly, "Why, no, ma'am, we did not, though unless he is in the habit of frequenting *modistes* and milliners, it would have been most unlikely."

The girls resumed their lessons almost immediately, for though Lady Harewood had already interviewed two prospective governesses, neither was found to suit. Another who had been recommended by a friend was to journey to Harewood Hall next month, when her present position would be terminated because her pupil was going to take up residence abroad with her diplomat-father.

Meanwhile Jessica spoke to Lord Harewood about Jemmy Dawson and begged to be allowed to take him to London. He could assist the groom, whom Burdock would have hired by the time of her return. At the same time Jessica could continue his lessons and improve his grammar in preparation for his entering a school. Lord Harewood was most agreeable to the proposal, even offering to put in a word in favor of the scheme with Jemmy's father.

The one servant that had been left for Jessica to hire on her own was an abigail. She would dearly have liked to take Rose, but she felt that after all Lady Harewood's kindness to her, it would be too bad of her to carry off one of her housemaids. However, during a talk with the girl, Rose said she would like to see London someday but she wouldn't want to live so far from her parents and her sister, so Jessica realized it was for the best that she had not spoken to Lady Harewood about the matter.

In the end she discovered a very pleasant country

girl by the name of Joan Stockley and liked her so well she engaged her on the spot.

Six weeks passed swiftly. Burdock wrote to inform her that the house in Portman Place was ready for her occupancy. The furniture and draperies were in place. The new wallpaper had been hung. The servants were engaged and the bottle green livery had been completed. Lady Wellby returned from Surrey to take her up to town.

Her parting with Claire and Delphie was a real wrench this time, for she knew she would never again come to this house save perhaps briefly as a guest. Miss Dunmoreton, a very sensible and well-informed woman, had been engaged as the new governess. Though both girls vowed she could never take their dear Miss Windom's place in their hearts, nevertheless she was filling Jessica's position; and Jessica was going off to a new life which held she knew not what, but which surely would be as different from her life here as this life had been from the one she had left more than a year ago, when she had departed from the dreary shelter of Monty Broyles's bleak roof.

Chapter Fourteen

Jessica was not two weeks in London before she was proclaimed an *original*. It came about from several callers overhearing a remark she made to Augustus Harling on the day after she had attended her first rout party.

It had been a modestly successful evening for Jessica, and Lady Wellby was well-enough satisfied. Though she would never be a diamond of the first water, she was in looks and manner engaging, with an attractive blend of confidence, good sense, and a readiness to be pleased. As she was neither a flirt nor a simpering schoolroom miss, she was seen to be something a little out of the ordinary style. The wondrous tale of her newfound fortune had somehow made its way about the social set and piqued much interest, also; those who engaged her in conversation, expecting to find a rustic, found instead a well-poised young woman.

Lady Wellby was gratified to discover her drawing room well populated with callers the next morning and was quite overwhelmed at the arrival of the Honorable Augustus Harling.

Jessica, looking quite pretty in a French muslin

gown of violet-blue, chanced to mention that she was hoping to persuade her trustee to allow her to purchase a phaeton, for she had been tooled through Hyde Park in one several days ago and found it most exhilarating.

"I am no whip though," she admitted, "for though I always lived in the country, I was never permitted to learn how to drive. Is that not shocking?"

"It is out of reason shocking," the Honorable Mr. Harling declared, "and shall be instantly remedied. If you will permit me, I will give you your first lesson this afternoon behind my grays."

There was a tiny moment of wondering silence as several visitors contemplated the magnitude of the offer. Harling's grays were only a trifle less well known than Harling himself, who was acknowledged to be one of the most notable whips in London. A member of the Four-Horse Club, he could drive to an inch. For him to make such an offer to a green girl was a surpassing mark of condescension.

"Oh, how much I should like that," Jessica said regretfully, "but I have already made an engagement with Iona Frayne to visit the Royal Academy. There are several new landscapes by Mr. Turner on exhibition now, you know."

The circle of faces around her could not have registered more shock had she tied her garter in public. Oddly, it was Tracey Damsetter who found his voice first. "B-b-but you c-c-could p-put her *off*, you know," he said in his customary stammer.

"Oh, no, what a shabby thing to put off one friend for the sake of another," Jessica said. "Mr. Harling has set me an example in kindness by offering to give me a driving lesson. He would surely think me unworthy of such notice were I to behave unkindly to Miss Frayne in order to avail myself of the lesson."

Mr. Harling bowed and said stiffly that he was sure Miss Wyndham set an example for them all in the nicety of her feelings, but he left soon afterward.

Of course the story spread like a brushfire and was all over town by the next day, whereupon Miss Wyndham was recognized as an authentic original. Her action did not, however, awaken admiration in every breast. The mamas of several young ladies of less countenance and smaller fortunes than Miss Wyndham were heard to opine that she had done it only to make herself interesting.

Among the girls of her acquaintance, some declared her to be the biggest goosecap in creation, while others applauded her as behaving just as she ought.

Among the young blades who admired skill with the ribbons above manners, the sentiment was expressed that Harling ought to give Miss Wyndham a sharp setdown and never notice her thereafter, but though Harling's handling of the reins was universally admired, his proud manner was not, and so Miss Wyndham also had partisans who declared it was refreshing to find a girl who didn't fall all over herself at the chance to pander to the fellow's vanity.

Meanwhile, during this episode when Jessica had repulsed—though ever so courteously—Mr. Harling's generous offer, Miss Iona Frayne had been sitting on the other side of the room chatting with an aquaintance and thus did not hear the conversation. When it was related to her afterward by Mr. Damsetter on his way out, she came hurrying over to Jessica. "Oh, Jessica, I wish you had not made me the cause of missing a driving lesson with Augustus Harling. Why, to be seen holding the reins of those grays of his would give you the *greatest* consequence. And we could have gone to the exhibition another time quite easily."

Jessica looked amused. "So that is what confers the *greatest* consequence, is it? Well, supposing I had overturned the phaeton? Then my reputation must have been irretrievably lost. Come, shall we make ready to go to the Royal Academy?"

Miss Iona Frayne was one of Jessica's earliest acquaintances in London. Her mother was a bosom bow of Lady Wellby's from long ago, and she had brought her daughter to call as soon as the newcomers were settled in.

"Tessa, how we have missed you. And what a delightful new face you have brought us to enliven the scene."

"Eliza," Lady Wellby said, kissing her friend. "How good of you to bring Iona. You have grown up since I saw you last, child. Come and let me make you known to my young friend, Jessica Wyndham."

Iona Frayne was an attractive girl several years older than Jessica. She was tall, with elegant carriage, and her hair was a pale silvery blonde. She was not quite a beauty, and yet there was great liveliness in her expression. Jessica warmed to her at once.

When they had made their how-do-you-dos, Miss Frayne said, "Mama, can you believe how Lady Pilchester's dreary Blue Saloon has been changed? Is it not delightful now?"

"Yes, it is quite different, and looks charming. Is this your work, Tessa?"

"Not at all. Jessica is responsible for all the changes, though I did just hint that Lady Pilchester's old drawing room draperies would give me a fit of the megrims if they were allowed to remain."

The four ladies conversed very comfortably, and their visit concluded with an invitation to Jessica to ride in the park with Iona on the morrow. As General Gormsley had chosen a very pretty little bay mare for her, she was happy to have a congenial companion to ride with.

Iona proved to be an agreeable friend. She introduced Jessica to a number of her acquaintances whom they met riding in Hyde Park at the same hour, and urged her to call with Lady Wellby at her own home in Russell Square. They also planned several outings, one of which was the fateful expedition to the Royal Academy.

Jessica thoroughly enjoyed the pictures, though Iona remained somewhat worried during the whole of the afternoon over what effect Jessica's spurning of Augustus Harling would have on her reputation. "For I know he is invited to the Fanhopes' ball tomorrow night. What if he should cut you? I should never forgive myself."

"Oh, fiddlesticks," Jessica cried, tired of the whole subject, which seemed to her a great piece of work over nothing. "What is the worst thing that can happen if he does? Perhaps I won't have any partners and will have to sit and talk all evening to the chaperones. Perhaps I will be a social outcast. I could bear up quite nicely under that, you know, Iona, for I did not come to London to become a society miss but to see a bit of the sights of interest. So I pray you will not worry your head anymore on that score."

Lady Wellby decreed that Jessica should wear her white sarcenet to the ball. "I know it is not your favorite gown," she said, "but it imparts such an air of innocence, and I think tonight to show a little of that quality will be no bad thing."

Though Jessica told herself stoutly that to be ostracized at the Fanhopes' ball was not of paramount importance in her life, still it would at the moment be somewhat embarrassing, so it was with a feeling of trepidation that she entered the brilliantly illuminated house. There was quite a crush, but to her gratification they had not been there above five minutes before she saw Iona coming toward her, accompanied by two gentlemen.

"Jessica," she said, smiling encouragement, "may I make known to you Lord Griffiths and my brother, Sir Richard Frayne."

Sir Richard topped his sister's height by a good six inches, and his hair was nearly as pale a gold as hers. Lord Griffiths was only a bit less tall, very elegantly dressed in a quiet way, and with direct blue eyes in his pleasing countenenace.

Both gentlemen immediately requested the pleasure of leading her out, which could not fail to relieve her mind, though she supposed Iona had arranged the matter. It was kind of her to do so, Jessica thought.

Before the evening was half over, it was apparent that she was not to be ostracized after all, as not one dance had she sat out until the waltz was played, and then in obedience to Lady Wellby's firm stricture, she had declined very prettily when asked, saying that she had not the approval of any of the patronesses of Almack's to do so, and that she therefore dared not put herself beyond the pale.

One of those patronesses was present at the Fanhopes' and had watched Jessica's deportment rather carefully during the evening. She was an old friend of Lady Wellby's and knew that her dear Tessa would be wanting to procure vouchers for her protégée. As a set ended, Lady Wellby brought Jessica over and presented her to Lady Cowper.

"Well, I have been hearing a good deal about you," she told the girl. "Do you intend to set all London by its ears?"

Startled, Jessica exclaimed, "Why, no, ma'am, and even if I had such an odd ambition, I can't suppose it would be in my power to do so."

"And yet it is the on-dit that you declined Mr. Harling's most flattering offer to teach you to drive."

"I was very sorry to do so, because it was very obliging of him, and I have heard him described as a top-sawyer, but the truth was I had made a previous engagement with Miss Frayne."

"And it did not occur to you to put her off?"

"No, ma'am, it did not. Nor did it occur to me that people would make such a piece of work over it. I'm sure there must be more important matters to challenge the mind than such a trifling episode."

"Well, Tessa, perhaps Miss Wyndham is, as people are saying, an original," Lady Cowper commented. "An original sometimes adds piquancy to the social scene. Then again, I have known some young ladies who were so carried away by their originality that they stepped beyond the line. However, I believe I like your little protégée, and I will give her a voucher for Almack's."

Lady Wellby's eyes twinkled. "That is most kind of you, Emily. Now run along, child; I believe you have promised this next dance to Mr. Mowbury. I want to sit here and have a little cose with Lady Cowper."

The next morning was sparkling clear, and Jessica was enjoying her ride in the park with Iona. After they had talked over the ball in general, Jessica said, "It was kind of you to introduce me to your brother and his friend. With two such eligible partners, I would not have been a complete wallflower, even if no one else had asked me to dance."

"Well, I did not ask them to lead you out, you know. I only made the introduction. I thought you might be glad of some new acquaintance, even if it was only Richard and Lord Griffiths. At any rate I knew you would have to meet Richard sometime, so it might as well have been soon as late."

"What can you mean, *only* your brother and Lord Griffiths?"

"Oh, we are not best of friends, my brother and I. When Papa died, he named Richard my guardian, and he has been puffed up with his importance ever since. He is continually meddling in my life. I know you will scarcely be able to credit it, but he has forever been trying to make a match between me and Lord Griffiths!"

"I suppose that is the way of guardians, is it not? And Lord Griffiths is a most personable gentleman."

"Humph!" Iona snorted in a rather unladylike way. "He is a fashionable fribble."

"Fashionable, certainly, but *fribble* I cannot allow," Jessica protested. "He talked to me most sensibly and entertainingly."

"About his horrid family seat, I make no doubt," Iona retorted. "Well, I have no desire to go and bury myself in the country where nothing is going on and I would have nothing useful to do."

"But, Iona, there is a great deal of good you could do in the country. You may not think so, having lived in London ever since your papa died, but aside from running your own household and raising a family, you could work to better the lot of the tenants. They would look to you, you know, for the relief of many ills if they knew you cared for their welfare."

"Well, I do not care for that sort of life at all. I would rather marry someone who is doing important work—a politican, for instance, who can shape the destiny of the whole country," she said with a sidewise glance at Jessica. "Do you go to Lady Buxton's soirée this evening? Good. There is always a great deal of talk there about the current debates. Lady Buxton is becoming very nearly as great a political hostess as Lady Holland, you know. That is what I should like— to live in London all year round and hold brilliant gatherings that would help my husband get ahead in his career. Being married to a mere title does not interest me in the least."

Jessica said no more on that head, but Iona's vehemence made her wonder if it was politics in general that exerted such a pull on her friend's mind or some politician in particular.

Lady Buxton's party was somewhat different from the other entertainments she had enjoyed. This pleased Jessica very well, for she was always open to new experience. She found some acquaintance there, but also many new faces.

Iona Frayne introduced her to a very tall young man with one of the handsomest faces she had ever seen. His dark brown hair was a little longer than custom decreed and worn carefully disheveled. His lips were full, his dark eyes had a strange, penetrating gleam, and his well-shaped chin held just a hint of a cleft. His white cravat was unstarched, his coat was of black velvet, and he wore no jewelry, not even a signet ring.

"This is Mr. Randall Jarvis, who is secretary to Lord Dumphries in the Exchequer," Iona said. "We look for great things of him."

"Miss Frayne is too kind," he said, and Jessica perceived that his voice was rich and well modulated.

Several of his friends joined the group at that moment, and the talk turned to the debates of the day in the House. Jessica found it all very fascinating and as the evening wore on could not but admire the way in which Lady Buxton drew out her guests so that the talk fairly sparkled. She could see why Iona felt the lure of becoming a political hostess, and yet if the only thing Iona held against Lord Griffiths was that he was not a politician, it seemed to Jessica that she was trying to choose a husband the wrong way round. Surely a man's profession should not be the first quality one looked for.

Early on the following day a note arrived from Mr. Potterby asking if he might send a visitor to call for a private interview. "Sir Jeremy Tidewell, late of the diplomatic service in India, has only just returned to England," he wrote. "I have acquainted him with your history, as he was a friend of your parents in Vienna. He is most eager to meet you and tell you what he knows of their circumstances."

Jessica, on reading the note which Lady Wellby had handed her, turned pale as wax. Then as color flooded back into her cheeks, she threw her arms around her friend. "Oh, I can scarcely speak. I want to know—I want to hear all, and yet—I am afraid."

"Oh, my dear child," Lady Wellby said kindly, "I am sure you have nothing to dread."

Jessica did not allow herself to fall into a fit of the vapors, yet she could not help an inner trembling. For so long she had held no image of her parents save that her father had deserted them and her mother had died in penury. Then she had learned that that was all falsehood, and she had been able to build happy dreams of parents who loved her.

But it was true that their families had disowned them. And it was true that they had given her to Monty Broyles. What if she learned something from

Sir Jeremy that she would rather have remained in ignorance of? Well, there was no turning back. She had begged Mr. Potterby to find someone from whom she could learn the truth.

Now he had done so, and she would have to face the consequences, whatever they might be. With her thoughts in turmoil she sat down at her little writing cabinet to pen a note to Mr. Potterby to say that she would expect Sir Jeremy on the morrow. Then she had to take herself sternly in hand and compose herself so that she might rub through this day's engagements with no one guessing what little command she had over her spirits.

Chapter Fifteen

"My dear child," Sir Jeremy said as he came forward and gripped both of her hands in a strong clasp. He seemed loth to let them go but stood looking down into her face until at last with misted eyes he turned away.

He blew his nose on a large linen handkerchief before finally saying to her, "You have a look of your mother about you, my dear, and yet your eyes are just the color of Jack's and your hair as well."

"I have wanted so much to meet someone who knew them well," Jessica said. "As you may know, until very recently I believed my father to have abandoned my mother and me, and I knew nothing whatever of their history. Now from Mr. Potterby I have heard the merest outline. But he says you were their friend."

"Indeed I was. I had a post with the embassy in Vienna. Jack and I had known one another at Oxford, and when your parents arrived in Vienna, we renewed our acquaintance."

"Mr. Potterby told me that my parents married to

disoblige their families and were cast off, both of them, and that is why they ran away to Vienna."

"Slowly, slowly, child. In the main that is true, but I shall tell you how it happened as Jack explained it to me. Your father was the younger son of a landed gentleman in Suffolk. His bent was for politics, but as to fortune, he possessed only the merest competence of his own. He tumbled top over tail into love with your mother, Marianne Mallowen, who was the ward of her uncle, a neighbor of Jack's family. She would come into a modest bit of money but not until she was twenty-five. Jack's father and Marianne's uncle had been on the outs for years—stiff-rumped, both of them. Some trifling affair had set them off and neither would back an inch. Jack's father objected to the proposed marriage on the grounds that Jack needed a girl of family and wealth who could be a grand hostess for him in his political career. Your mother had a merry heart and laughing ways, and he did not think she was the right wife for a politician—or so he said, though Jack always felt his true objection was that Marianne was not rich enough to overcome old Wyndham's dislike of Marianne's uncle. Also there was the daughter of a family friend he had always hoped to see Jack marry.

"Both young people stood firm, their attachment remaining unaltered until Marianne was of age. There was still no reasoning with his father or her uncle, so they married despite all objections, gave up all intercourse with their families, and went to live in a cottage where Jack says they were happy as larks entertaining any of their old friends who came to see them.

Then after a year an aunt of Jack's died and unaccountably left him her money. She had met Marianne and liked her, and though she never gave a hint of what she intended to do, suddenly they found themselves with a respectable income.

"This provoked Jack's father and he was more bitter against them than before, throwing up more obstacles than ever in Jack's way should he wish to return to political life, so, tired of the wrangling, they simply cut all ties with home and went to travel on the Continent, settling at last in Vienna.

"Eventually Marianne came into her own money. They had a very lively home, entertaining any English who came to the capital with whom they had any acquaintance and making scores of new friends. Your mother was a very accomplished pianist, and they had musical evenings of great brilliance. Your father made himself most useful to the embassy. After nearly ten years of marriage, their happiness was complete when you were born. There were never two prouder parents. I can remember seeing you when you were scarcely out of leading strings, riding between them in their curricle wearing a velvet coat and hood trimmed with white fur all around your face."

Jessica's eyes were brimming but she said not a word as Sir Jeremy paused reminiscently and cleared his throat again.

"Meanwhile matters had taken a strange turn at home. Jack's sister had married and gone to Scotland. His mother died, leaving the greater share of her own money to Jack. Then his brother was killed in a coaching accident. Old Wynham was completely cut up over it. There was no title involved and the property was not entailed, so since he had no son but Jack to inherit, and he still could not forgive Jack, he sold the property and went to live out his last years in London, but he was a broken man.

"Marianne's uncle died and left his money to her, so this couple that had started with naught but a smile to live upon was, through the odd falling out of fate, becoming richer and richer. Then old Wyndham died and, surprisingly enough, in his will he divided his money between his two surviving children, so in the end he must have forgiven Jack after all, though he never communicated with him before he died.

"They could have come back to London, of course, but they were happy in Vienna. The life they were living was brilliant and exciting. I never knew a happier couple."

Sir Jeremy reached out and squeezed Jessica's hand.

"Then tragedy came. Your lovely mother contracted influenza and died of it. Your father, ill with it himself, was crazy with grief. He felt sure he would die too, and to tell the truth I think he did not care to go on living without Marianne.

"As it chanced, a connection of his wife's, a distant cousin, was in Vienna at the time. It was not his first visit. I had met him before and thought him an encroaching fellow. He was horse-mad, I remember. But your parents were too kind not to entertain him as royally as they did everyone.

"I had been out of the city and only arrived back in time to rush to his house and find your father very near the end. He told me he knew he was dying and that he was going to send you to his sister in Scotland, and that Broyles was going to take you back to London. He said he believed his sister did not even know she had a niece, as there had been no communication between the two for years. 'But Dora was always a good-hearted, sensible girl and she'll look after my poor, sweet Jessica,' he told me.

"Sick as he was, he had written letters which he showed to me, and he had the documents proving your birth. I remember there was a letter to his sister commending you to her care. There was also a letter introducing Broyles to his lawyers, as it was his intention that Broyles take you to London, where he would acquaint the legal firm of the circumstances and deliver Jack's will, in which he left everything to you to be paid on your majority, with such allowance meanwhile as his lawyers deemed suitable.

"Of course he was very ill when he made these arrangements, and I was very much shocked and distraught to see my friend at such a pass. I have searched my mind to discover if there was any ambiguity in the letters, and I can only suppose that all was not made as clear as it should have been. Broyles apparently destroyed the letter to Jack's sister. The one introducing him must not have made clear enough that Jack had given you into Broyles's care only for the duration of the trip back to England. Apparently without the epistle to his sister, the second letter gave the impression that Jack had intended Broyles to become your guardian. I blame myself very much that it did not occur to me that such a thing could come about, but of course neither Jack nor I could have imagined Broyles to be such a scoundrel.

"I was posted almost immediately to Constantinople, then to Tunis, afterward spending some years in India. Before I left Vienna I did contact the Austrian nurse who accompanied you on the journey, and she assured me that you had arrived safely in London and that Broyles had hired an English nanny for you and arranged for her own passage back to Vienna. It is to my eternal regret that I never contacted Jack's sister during all these years to make sure of your welfare."

"Oh, no, sir, why should you have done such a thing?" Jessica cried, seeing that he was sunk into a profound melancholy. "You are in no way to blame. No one could have suspected such perfidy from my cousin. Certainly my father did not, and he was better acquainted with him than you."

"But when I think of the many years you were deprived of your rightful due, living with the bare necessities of life and none of its elegances, it makes my blood boil."

"Well, sir, if the truth were told, I own that I do resent the fact that Monty's daughters were living on my money, all the while treating me like a poor destitute who ought to be grateful for their castoff clothes and the very bread in my mouth. But to give them their due, I suppose that they did not know the truth of the matter. However, I shall never forgive Monty for allowing me to grow up believing I was not even legitimate. But as for the rest, perhaps I should not have liked it in Scotland after all. And if I had not been brought up at Gray Gables, I should never have known my dear Lady Sarah and Mr. Raynes. My life was not all grimness, you know. Pretty clothes and toys are superficial things, after all. What they gave me was more important and more enduring—affection and a good education. Perhaps I should have had neither with my aunt in Scotland, and if that were the case then all the luxury in the world would have been meaningless."

Very much moved, Sir Jeremy said, "You are a good girl, my dear. Your parents would have been proud of you."

With tears in her eyes she said, "I can never thank you enough for coming to see me. I feel that in telling me about them, you have given me back the most important thing that was denied me these past years."

That evening Jessica seemed to Lady Wellby to be glowing with an inner light. "How glad I am that we are not expected anywhere tonight," she said. "I want to stay alone and hug my happiness to me."

Before she went to bed her candle guttered low as she poured out Sir Jeremy's whole story in a letter to Lady Sarah. She could not bear to cross her lines; she wanted every word standing out clearly so she filled several sheets, thinking as she folded it and affixed the wafer that she trusted Lady Sarah would think the good news worth the extra sixpence she would have to pay.

The next day she and her abigail, Joan Stockley, were just leaving the house when a smart curricle pulled up in the front. Iona's brother, Sir Richard, held the reins. Lord Griffiths jumped down and made her a graceful bow. "Your servant, Miss Wyndham. I see we have timed our arrival badly. Richard and I hoped to give ourselves the pleasure of a visit with you, but I see that you have another engagement."

She gave him a straightforward smile. "Yes, I have, and I pray you will not tell anyone what it is, for I most earnestly wish to avoid any more talk about my being an *original*. Such nonsense! But I really cannot put off this engagement, for I have promised to take Master Jemmy Dawson to the Tower of London."

"Lucky Master Dawson," Lord Griffiths said. "Is he a young relative of yours?"

"No, he is my student and also my stable boy for the moment, though I hope he will soon be entered in a school. He is the most exceptional little chap, and he has been good as gold about keeping to his books, so I have promised him this treat, which is an appropriate one as we have lately been studying English history."

"Would Master Dawson think it too encroaching if we begged to join your party?" Sir Richard asked. "I think I have not visited the tower since I was a lad myself."

She looked to see if he were serious and could find no mockery in his eyes. Lord Griffiths's face, too, held only friendly interest. "Well, if you truly wish it," she said, "I would be very pleased to have you come. But we shall have to ride in my carriage, which is being brought around this minute."

Sir Richard turned his curricle over to his groom to be taken home, and both gentlemen greeted Jemmy gravely on introduction.

They had a very gay time of it at the tower. Jessica was in possession of all sorts of historical insights which both the young men claimed to be new to them, and Jemmy kept them amused with his bloodthirsty insistence on seeing the exact spots where various heads had rolled and bones had been disinterred.

They enjoyed some ices afterward, and Jessica felt herself very much in charity with both men, whose easy company had helped make the outing such an agreeable one.

Soon afterward Jessica and Iona made a shopping expedition to the Pantheon Bazaar. Though Jessica had thought that there was not one single thing in all the world that she needed, she did discover a reticule in a shade of celestial blue which she thought would exactly match a pair of her kid slippers, and a silver rose that would look charmingly at the waistline of her white sarcenet, not to mention a new pair of evening gloves in palest pink satin.

Iona outdid her friend in the number of parcels she stowed into the carriage for the drive home. As the horses clattered along, she said, "Did I hear Lady Wellby say that Lord Markham was to be invited to your rout party tomorrow night?"

"Yes . . . He is the brother of Lady Harewood, whose daughters I was governess to. He has been away from London since the season began and is only just returned, I believe," she said carefully. "Are you acquainted with him?"

There was a little constraint in Iona's manner. Then she said, "He and my brother are monstrously great friends. And Lord Griffiths is of his set also." Her curled lip and her tone of voice spoke eloquently of her feelings toward that set.

Jessica gave a little laugh. "Not everyone is a villain merely because he is your brother's friend. And I think you wrong Lord Griffiths, too. I have become better acquainted with him, and I like him very well. I think he is kind and sensible and entertaining—and certainly *not* a fribble." She smiled coaxingly at Iona as she spoke, but the other girl refused to be drawn.

"Oh, I grant you that he and my brother can assume charming manners when they choose. But to be forever under Richard's thumb is the most oppressing thing. I cannot think whatever possessed Papa to name Richard as my trustee. I shall be on the *shelf* before I come into my inheritance. I shall be five-and-twenty. That is four more years of making and scraping on the most niggardly allowance. And it is of no use at all to apply to Mama, as she is always run off her feet. She has not the smallest notions of economy."

Jessica surpressed a smile because it did not seem to her that Iona showed any such notions either. "Perhaps you will marry before then," she said. "You will soon be of age."

"Unless I marry Griffiths, my brother won't open the purse strings wide enough for me to buy bride clothes. Worse, I do not doubt that he would find some way to prevent me altogether—carry me off to his estate in Northumberland and keep me prisoner. He could do it, you know. The servants are all in his pay."

"Of course they are in his pay," Jessica protested.

"There is nothing sinister in that. It is his house, after all."

"Even my own abigail is his choice," Iona flashed out. "He dismissed my Letty two years ago only because—oh, no matter, but it was for a trifling reason. You do not know what it is like to have a brother wishing to dictate your every move to you."

"No, indeed I do not," Jessica agreed. "But I must own I think you do not either, for I cannot believe your brother dictated the purchase of two parasols, three new scarves, and a bunch of feathers, not to mention a whole rainbow of ribbons and a painted fan, all in one day."

Iona's lips twitched and she allowed herself to be diverted. She opened one of the parcels and extracted the pink parasol with the rosebuds sprinkled on it. "Isn't this the most delicious trifle? Oh, I do hope tomorrow is a sunny day."

Chapter Sixteen

The rout was to be the first entertainment Lady Wellby had held in her protégée's honor. Earlier on she had mentioned the possibility of a ball, but Jessica had demurred. "Oh, please, ma'am, a ball for me? I would feel a great deal too *coming*." She did see the force of Lady Wellby's suggestion that they must do something to repay the people who had been so obliging as to invite *her* to routs and drums and dress parties and balls, but her first suggestion—that they give a musical evening—did not find favor with Lady Wellby.

"For you know, my love, that some of the very people whose hospitality you most wish to repay would not enjoy that sort of thing, however much they might claim to be music lovers. Though of course later in the season you may certainly hold one if you like. But I do think a rout party would be best, with card tables set up in the Red Saloon, and the drawing room cleared for perhaps fifteen or twenty couples to dance. And of course a light supper laid on in the dining room."

To this plan Jessica finally gave her approval, and

indeed on the morning of the rout, she seemed in quite unusually high spirits. It was not that her manner was ever less than cheerful, and she took an eager interest in almost every situation in which she found herself, but still in many ways her spirit was a serious one and her humor more inclined to drollery than gaiety.

But as this day wore on, her color was high, and she seemed almost compelled to a perfect frenzy of activity. Lady Wellby hoped she was not sickening. When she had asked for the fourth time if Lady Wellby was *quite* sure they had ordered enough ices, that lady said with some asperity, "I am absolutely certain. And I think you had best stop rearranging those poor flowers or they will soon begin to lose their petals. Indeed I think it would be wise if you retired to your room to rest before your nervous energy wears you down. You don't want to look hagged at your own party, do you?"

"Oh, fiddle," Jessica retorted.

Lady Wellby was turning over some notes that had arrived. "Oh, too bad. Here is a message from Lord Markham. He regrets that a previous engagement will make it impossible for him to attend our party this evening. Eugenia Harewood is so delightful that I was quite hoping to become better acquainted with her brother, as I know him only slightly. But I daresay now that he is in London we shall run into him somewhere."

She attended to the rest of the messages and was pleased to see that her words had had some good effect on her protégée. Jessica's manner had calmed to its customary propriety, and in fact presently she said that if Lady Wellby did not need her, she would take her advice and retire to her room.

"That's a good girl. And do lie down upon your bed for an hour or so. Run along now, my dear."

But when Jessica reached her bedchamber it was not to lie down but to stand before her mirror staring at herself. Perhaps she did look hagged, she thought, though it hardly mattered. She regarded herself critically. Her hair was somewhat disheveled, and she wondered now for the first time if her coiffure was really becoming to her or if she should let her hair grow out and twist it into a knot that would make her look older. Her skin did not satisfy her, either. Too many summers rambling about without a sunshade had left her complexion lacking that pale creaminess that was so desirable. And her nose, of course—that was quite beyond redemption.

Joan had already laid out her clothes. She wound a silver hair fillet absently through her fingers and stared at the rest with indifference.

By the time Jessica took her place to greet her guests, Lady Wellby was relieved to see that she was looking more herself, not displaying any of the feverish gaiety of the afternoon. It would have been too bad to have to chide her for behaving like a hoyden at her own party. There was no fear of that, however, and indeed as the evening wore on, it seemed as if she were almost *too* calm. It crossed Lady Wellby's mind that her manner might be simply masking nervousness, but she dismissed that notion as it seemed more and more evident that Jessica was simply going through the motions in a somewhat perfunctory way.

When the last guest had finally departed, she said, "Well, my dear, did you enjoy yourself?"

Jessica was looking rather wan but roused herself to say prettily, "Oh, indeed, ma'am. Everyone was so kind. And all your arrangements were perfection. You are so good to take such trouble with me."

"It gives me great pleasure to do so, but I think you have tired yourself. Go to bed now, child." Left alone, she wondered if in spite of all the hopes of her cousin Sarah, of Eugenia Harewood, and of herself, Jessica was too much of a bluestocking to care more than the snap of her fingers for the social scene. It would be too bad. Not, of course, that she would want the child to let the round of partying go to her head. But she seemed quite as excited by a visit to the British Museum or to Hookham's Library as she did by a ball. And if she lost interest altogether in going about in society, where would she find the proper husband?

So far she did not think Jessica showed signs that her heart had in any way been touched. Richard Frayne would be an unexceptionable match, and she seemed disposed to be friendly toward him, but so far, not more. Did she think him too old, perhaps?

She had been very astute—more astute than Lady Wellby could have hoped—in recognizing the pretensions of several gazetted fortune hunters who had made a set at her. Even Dennis Milbanke, who had such charm that mamas of innocent heiresses had been known to turn pale and fall into the vapors when he so much as looked at one of their daughters—even Mr. Milbanke had only received an appraising look from Jessica; she had sent him on his way coolly without showing the slightest sign of falling victim to his coaxing ways.

Well, perhaps she had not met the right man yet. The season was still young. Blake Endicott had seemed quite besotted with her tonight, though she hadn't seemed to notice. Perhaps her odd humors today only meant she was coming down with an epidemic cold or some such ailment. Mr. Endicott would have time to attract her attention later.

The drawing room next morning held a gratifying number of floral offerings as well as visitors. Mr. Endicott was one of the first to arrive, along with Tracey Damsetter, who, though he had been shocked at her treatment of Augustus Harling, had decided he admired Miss Wyndham after all and had discovered that somehow in her calm and forthright presence he seemed to stammer less.

Lord Griffiths and Sir Richard Frayne stopped in for a brief visit, and Randall Jarvis, looking rather magnificent in his blue coat despite the studied casualness of his shirt points and cravat, appeared shortly after they had departed.

Jessica was wearing a cambric round gown in a soft olive shade with the very high waist and tiny puffed sleeves suitable to her youth, and yet its rather unusual color and extreme simplicity gave it a certain air of sophistication. She seemed more in command of her spirits this morning and was carrying on an animated conversation with Mr. Jarvis and several others when the butler announced Lord Markham.

After hesitating for one arrested moment, she excused herself, saying that an old acquaintance whom she had not seen in some months had arrived.

He did not possess himself of her hand for more than the briefest touch, but he was so long in replying to her greeting that she began to feel very odd indeed. At last he said, "No need to ask if London agrees with you. One glance is enough to show that it has put you into fine frame."

She made a little gesture with her hand, dismissing the compliment. "Oh, as to that—*et genus et formam regina pecunia donat*, as Horace said." And then before he had a chance to speak, she said in rather pedantic condescension but with a mocking twinkle in her eyes, "That means, 'Money, like a queen, gives both rank and beauty,' you know."

If she had expected him to take instant umbrage she was mistaken, for he did not rise to the fly but only said quietly, "Yes, I do know, but it is quite inappropriate, because money was not needed to confer either of those benefits."

For a moment she was quite bereft of rational thought, and then it came to her that he had put on his London manners. She had heard that he was a practiced flirt who had left a score of bruised vanities behind, though in fairness it had never been suggested that he went beyond the line in giving any young lady hopes of something more permanent. If he was trying to get up a flirtation with her now, he would be disappointed. She was not such a green girl as to be taken in, *pas si bête*. She thought she liked him better when he was ripping up at her. At least then he had seemed honest.

"You must come and greet Lady Wellby and some of my friends," she said and led him across the room.

"We were so sorry you could not join us last evening," Lady Wellby said. "I like your sister so much. I have been looking forward to renewing our acquaintance."

"I regret that I was unable to accept your kind invitation," he said rather stiffly.

He seemed not too pleased to greet her other callers and quite ignored the number of posies that had been ranged about the room. He did not stay long, but when he took his leave of Jessica, he said, "I have not previously had an opportunity to felicitate you on your change of circumstance. It must have seemed a dream come true."

"Oh, no," Jessica disclaimed. "I never had such dreams. I fear that I am not at all imaginative."

"I am very happy for you," he said in such a grave way that after he had gone she stood thinking: "If that is the way he looks when he is happy, I should hate to see him sad." And then such an astonishing notion crossed her mind that she stood quite still, seeing nothing for a moment until she finally gave herself a mental shake and told herself not to be an idiot. "I have just said that I am not imaginative. It would be foolish beyond anything to begin to imagine things at this late date."

Lord Markham had come to London with a certain degree of reluctance, but he had drawn out all his excuses for staying away at such length that it would begin to look very odd if he did not make his appearance soon.

It had been his intention to call in Portman Place as soon as possible to get his first meeting with Jessica past him before he was obliged to come upon her in a crowded room.

He did not know for a certainty that she was going about in society, but he had cut his wisdoms long ago and he realized the significance of Lady Tessa Wellby's presence as her chaperone. It was obvious that between them Lady Sarah and his dratted sister had schemed to pitchfork Jessica into the ton. Lady Wellby was just the sort of well-born woman, who knew everyone and who was invited everywhere, to accomplish it.

On his first evening in town, he had dined at his club, where he ran into his friends Richard Frayne and William Griffiths. They chatted idly, passing along a number of on-dits about his acquaintance, and then Frayne said, "But I suspect you have stolen a march on us all, as you are already acquainted with the season's original, are you not?"

The viscount raised his eyebrows.

"Jessica Wyndham," Frayne explained. "She said she used to be Eugenia's governess. She wasn't shamming it, was she? She has such a droll way, one never knows what she might take it into her head to say."

"Yes, she was with Eugenia for a while, and I am somewhat acquainted with her," he said in a reserved way. "I trust she is getting on well."

"Very thick with my sister, the little Wyndham is. That's the only thing I know to her discredit."

"Coming it a bit too strong," Griffiths said reprovingly.

"Oh, there's no harm in Iona, I'll grant, but we always chafe one another. She's never forgiven me for being appointed her guardian. She's perfectly sure if Papa were alive or if he had appointed a *reasonable* guardian, she'd be allowed to squander her inheritance and to run off with the first here-and-thereian who turned her head. Of course she is fair and far out there. Papa would have kept a tighter rein on her than I ever do. I don't raise the dust when she finds herself under the hatches before quarter day. Stands to reason I can't, with Mama leading her on."

"I'm sure your sister is too intelligent ever to run seriously into debt," Lord Griffiths said. "Has it ever occurred to you she sometimes runs close to the wind just to try your patience?"

"Oh, yes, she's needle-witted enough in some ways. And I give her full marks for taking an interest in something beyond clothes and tittle-tattle, but she's not up to snuff in choosing her friends. Some of those politicians she fancies are dashed smoky—Randall Jarvis, for one. I cannot like him as an acquaintance for my sister," he said rather grimly, "and yet he is received everywhere. Well, perhaps her new little friend from the country will be a good influence on Iona, unless Iona turns out to be a bad influence on her. Though the little Wyndham seems to have her head screwed on right. She gave Milbanke the roundabout

205

quick enough. Surprised him the devil a bit. Had thought she was so green she'd be ripe for the plucking."

"Mixing your metaphors a bit, aren't you?" Griffiths inquired with a grin.

They went on to recount a number of stories regarding Jessica, all unknowing that their friend listened as a man divided, half of him proud of her success in making her way, the other half in despair because it was obvious she needed nothing from him.

Later when the invitation card to the rout party arrived, he decided he would not attend. She had no need of his support, certainly. If it would be an exaggeration to say that she had taken London by storm, still in a few short weeks she had secured a place for herself, earning the admiration and respect of such men as Griffiths and Frayne. No, he would not appear at the rout but he would pay a courtesy call the next day. . . . Now having paid his call, he went away from the house feeling she had given him a leveler indeed.

Her dress, her coiffure, were in the first stare of à la modality and yet somehow made her look even younger than when she had attired herself so primly as a governess. He remembered Salford's words that she was not a beauty, and it was true, but she had something beyond beauty. There was liveliness and intelligence in that face, and a sort of well-bred grace. It was, in short, the only face that had the power to touch his heart. And yet for all her poise and social adeptness, he looked back with a wistful tenderness to the moment he had seen her sitting at Monty Broyles's hearth in her ill-fitting dress and shaggy hair, looking like a poor waif. If only he had had the sense to recognize her at that moment for the love he had long despaired of finding—if only he had gone to her then and put his arms around her and sworn to take care of her always.

Then he had to smile at the thought of the sensation that action would have aroused there in the ugly drawing room at Gray Gables.

She did not need anything from him now, but he would keep an eye on her all the same. She had had the wit to see through the pretentions of several fortune hunters, but she was only a green girl, after all. Perhaps she would have need of him yet, if only to send another April Squire on his way.

Chapter Seventeen

Having heard the famous story of Augustus Harling's rejected driving lesson, it occurred to Lord Markham that this was one area in which he might be of some small service to Jessica.

Upon making the offer, he was somewhat chagrined to discover that he was far from being the first to try to repair that omission, and yet she seemed well enough pleased to drive out with him, which emboldened him to suggest they drive all the way to Richmond Park.

"Oh, yes, I would like that," she said, "for though I haven't disgraced myself, I am still the merest whipster and I do so want to learn to hold the reins in form and take a curve to a nicety. And do you think you could teach me to catch my thong over my head?"

He laughed and allowed that it was not beyond the realm of possibility.

On the appointed day she was looking very charming in a gypsy hat tied under her chin with rosy ribbons. She put her chestnuts through their paces very creditably for one who had so lately learned to drive. In the park he began her lesson, amused by the seriousness of her concentration. Eventually, certain that she must be tiring, he had suggested that he take the reins.

"Just a bit longer," she said. "I believe I am *almost* on the point of catching the thong properly." Her attention all on her whip, she rounded a corner too wide and came to grief grazing the wheel of a curricle going in the opposite direction.

With a bellow of rage the driver of the other vehicle leaped down to examine his wheel, then rounded on Jessica with a look of fury. As Jessica sat quaking, Lord Markham jumped down too and took measure of his adversary, a very young gentleman dressed in a driving coat with above a dozen capes and a cluster of whip points thrust through his buttonhole.

The viscount examined Jessica's wheel and then said loftily, "Fortunately little harm was done, so a simple apology to the lady will suffice."

The youth's face empurpled as he sputtered, "Apol—*apologize!* For what, pray? I gave over so far I was nearly ditched. The lady might almost have been trying to push me off the road. It was her fault entirely."

The viscount's brows rose to an astonishing high. "*Trying* to ditch you! This gentlewoman was trying to push you off the road? And what was the reason, pray, for this murderous assault on your person? Does she have cause to wish the earth rid of your presence? Or perhaps she merely took exception to the cut and color of your driving coat."

For a moment the boy could not even speak; then

he said frigidly, "I do not accuse her of anything more than bad driving."

"You—accuse—*my* pupil—of bad driving!" He raised his quizzing glass and studied the hapless youth at length. "You are Farnsworth, are you not? I remember when your name came before the Four-Horse Club. I am Markham."

Mr. Farnsworth was thrown into confusion. An aspirant to the prestigious Four-Horse Club scarcely dared to make an enemy of Lord Markham. "Well, if that's how it is," he said in confusion. "I didn't realize the lady was having a driving lesson."

"You misunderstand me," the viscount said coldly. "When I called her my pupil, I meant that it was under my tutelage that she learned to drive. She is far beyond the need for instruction *now*, as she can drive to an inch. And if the Four-Horse Club were open to young ladies, *she* would have had no trouble gaining admittance. But we will say no more on that head."

Mr. Farnsworth muttered something that might have been an explanation, an apology, or a further complaint, but it was so confused that it was impossible to say where his intention lay. The viscount gave him a curt nod of dismissal and climbed back into the phaeton.

Jessica started off her horses at a spanking pace, and when they had distanced themselves from the scene of the mishap, she said, "Oh, do please take the reins, as I think I am going to fall into a strong spasm." Laughter gurgled forth from her lips. "That poor boy. Such a peal as you rang over him! And it was all quite my fault. You are shameless."

"Nonsense," the viscount said. "The young puppy will be all the better for a set-down. Besides, if he *will* wear a coat like that, no one could be blamed for running him off the road."

"And telling him that I can drive to an inch. What a plumper! It's enough to put him off women for life."

"I find that Mr. Farnsworth's attitude toward women does not concern me overmuch," the viscount said insouciantly.

It was the boy Jemmy Dawson who took the horses when they arrived back at Portman Place, and this reminded Markham guiltily of his long-ago promise to look into the matter of a school for the child. At the time of Jessica's request, he had made some inquiries, but none of the schools he investigated had seemed to fit the bill for dealing with a previously unschooled country lad, and so he had written to her.

The fact that she had brought him to town indicated that she had not given up her plans for him, and no doubt even at the height of the season she was still finding time to give him lessons. She was indeed an original, little Jessica Windom.

Several days later he was admitted to her drawing room to find Iona Frayne with her. After some minutes of conversation it seemed apparent that Miss Frayne had no intention of leaving, so he said, "I had something I particularly wanted to discuss, Miss Wyndham. I have looked more fully into the matter of schools for Jemmy Dawson, and I believe I have discovered one that may please you."

"Oh, but that's all settled," Miss Frayne said airily.

"Mr. Randall Jarvis took care of it and Jemmy is entered for the coming term."

"Yes, that is so," Jessica said. "It was kind of you to trouble yourself. I ought to have told you there was no further need, but to tell the truth I supposed you had forgotten it long since."

He was deeply mortified, a feeling which was not assuaged when Miss Frayne said, "We are going to the Upper House today to hear Lord Dumphries's speech. Mr. Jarvis wrote it, of course. He is such a brilliant writer. How we look forward to the day when he can deliver speeches himself, as his voice is so particularly suited to oratory."

"I will not detain you further, then," the viscount said stiffly and bowed himself out.

When Jessica and Iona came away from the House that afternoon, Iona was very nearly in transports. "Oh, do let us walk for a bit in Hyde Park," she begged. "I cannot bear anything so tame as sitting and drinking a cup of tea."

As they headed down a shaded walk, she said, "Was it not the finest speech imaginable? Was it not stirring?"

Jessica considered. "It had merit, but I did not think the point about the agricultural reform was well taken."

"The agricultural—oh, goosecap, not Lord Henley's speech; I mean Lord Dumphries's."

"Oh, yes, I did enjoy it very well. Lord Dumphries has such a striking delivery, the way he clears his throat after every period. Wondering if he will be able to go on keeps one fairly on the edge of one's chair."

"You are roasting me, you wicked one," Iona admonished, squeezing her friend's arm. "But truly, was it not brilliant?"

"I can see we will come to dagger-drawing if I don't agree, so I may as well do so at once."

"Oh, if only Randall could have read the speech himself! His voice is so powerfully affecting and his appearance is all that would make one trust him. He will go far in political life without a doubt!"

"Randall?" Jessica said, surprised at her friend's use of Mr. Jarvis's first name.

Iona turned suddenly toward her. "Oh, Jessica, say that I can entrust you with a confidence! But I need not ask. I know I can. You are a loyal friend and no gabble-monger."

"Of course I am your friend, Iona, but I wish to pry into no secrets," she said uneasily.

"But I want you to know. Mr. Jarvis—Randall—and I are secretly promised to one another!"

She spoke in thrilling accents, but Jessica knew a sense of dismay. "Secretly? But why, Iona? Why must it be secret?"

"Because of my horrid brother. Can you wonder I am out of charity with him?"

"Has Mr. Jarvis spoken to him?"

"There was no need. I spoke to him myself two whole years ago, when we first knew we were irrevocably in love. But Richard is so cruel he wouldn't even entertain such a thought. He utterly refused to give his consent and said I was mad to think he'd increase my allowance so as to support a husband."

It crossed Jessica's mind that it was an odd start for Iona to have approached her brother rather than leaving it to Mr. Jarvis, to whom that task properly belonged.

"He threatened to send me off to Northumberland at once if I did not give Randall up, and so I had to pretend to comply, distasteful as it was not to be aboveboard, for in Northumberland I should never have been able to see him at all. At least this way we can meet in company. Richard comforts himself with the belief I have given up all thoughts in that direction, and he is forever pushing me at Lord Griffiths, which would be laughable if it did not make me so angry. I cannot bear his arrogant interference."

"I'm sorry," Jessica said quietly. "As you know, I like Lord Griffiths and thought that you were enjoying his company at the theater party the other evening, but I would of course not have included him had I known his presence disturbed you."

"Oh, I do not dislike him; it is only that I do not wish Richard to think he can tell me whom to marry. He has always been overbearing. It is only his abominable prejudice that keeps him from appreciating Randall. Richard despises him because he wasn't born hosed and shod. I swear you would think Randall smelled of the shop, the way my brother behaves. But it is not true. His father was perfectly respectable, only rather poor—a younger son of a country gentleman with only a small farm given into his care. And Randall is a younger son, too, so he has even less, but it doesn't matter because he will have a brilliant career. Why, he could be anything. I make no doubt he could rise as high as—oh, as Chancellor of the Exchequer!"

There was a flush on her face that made her look very pretty. "And I will marry him someday no matter if Richard starves me meanwhile. But how cruel he is to make us wait and waste these years when we could be so happy together. I have loved him faithfully for two whole years, but such a thing does not matter to my brother."

"Oh," Jessica cried, much struck. "How like my parents' situation it is!"

"Your parents?" Iona asked.

"Yes, my father too was destined for a career in politics. And my mother's guardian would not give his consent."

"What happened?" Iona breathed.

"They waited until my mother was of age, married, and were cast off by their families."

"Ohh, and were they happy?"

"Yes, they were very happy, though my father gave up his career because they had no expectations."

"They counted the world well lost," Iona quoted in an exalted tone.

"I believe they did. But then they came into some money and went abroad. And it was the strangest thing—they inherited more and more and became quite rich."

"You see," Iona said, "they eventually triumphed over prejudice, and so shall we, only Randall will not have to give up his career because my brother cannot keep my inheritance from me past my twenty-fifth year."

"That is true," Jessica agreed, "and if you love each other enough to wait—"

Iona seized her arm, a strange light in her eyes. "But why should we wait? I am now turned twenty-one. We would have to make and scrape for the next four years, but eventually all would come right—as it did for your parents!"

Jessica felt herself infected with her friend's enthusiasm. "Then perhaps you should be open with your brother. Let him know of the constancy of your feelings—"

"Oh, no. He would find a way to prevent it. I told you he would not scruple to cut off my allowance entirely and send me into Northumberland in order to prevent my marrying Randall. But if we could contrive a way to carry it off without his knowing until it was too late—I daresay we would have to live in some dingy lodging for the next four years, but we would be happy—just like your mama and papa."

"I beg you will not do anything rash," Jessica said in alarm, sorry now that she had mentioned her parents' story and put ideas into Iona's head.

"Oh, no, I will do nothing rash," Iona promised. "This will take a good deal of thought."

And with that Jessica had to be content.

The pleasurable round of gaiety continued. Lady Wellby held a Venetian breakfast, which was thought by all to be a great success. Lady Frayne's turtle party was equally well received.

Jessica had the felicity, when attending Almack's Assemblies, of having her hand bespoken for every dance. Lord Markham's absence at most of the Assemblies was noted and puzzled over in many quarters. But on one occasion he came, looking the picture of quiet elegance in his satin knee breeches and well-cut coat, and claimed Jessica's hand for a waltz. "For I know you must have been granted permission by one of the patronesses to perform it long since."

She admitted it was so, and he led her out, performing the turns with such grace that it fairly took her breath away, but he was so silent that after a time she was prompted to inquire if anything were amiss. He seemed to draw his thoughts back and said, "Oh, no. I was just thinking that your gown is the color of a new willow tree and it put me in mind of the lines

*Make me a willow cabin at your gate,
and call upon my soul within the house."*

She felt a strange fluttering in her chest. When he spoke no further, she said lightly, "Very pretty, my lord, but I thought we had agreed to wear our learning like a watch and keep it in our pocket."

He smiled then. "Oh, no, Miss Wyndham. You and Chesterfield agreed upon it. I never had such a notion. Indeed I take every opportunity that arises to puff off my knowledge."

That made her laugh and they finished the dance in good accord but a little later she saw that he had left the Assembly without asking her to dance again.

Chapter Eighteen

Balls and routs and dress parties were very agreeable to a girl who had never been given the opportunity for frivolity, and Jessica also took keen delight in riding her own well ribbed up mare and driving a bang-up turnout of prime goers. An evening at the theater was pleasing beyond words, and the ready availability of paintings and curios and books old and new could not fail to satisfy her eager mind.

Still she did not think to spend the rest of her life in idleness (though many of her acquaintance would have acquitted her of that charge on the basis of the amount of study and reading she found time for). She had come to consider it possible that London might be the place she would choose to live permanently, perhaps renting a small cottage in Staffordshire during the summer months. However, she knew she would not be content to drift for long simply partaking of the entertainments available to a girl of substance.

While Mr. Jarvis was the one who had discovered the school which Jemmy would attend, Jessica had visited it several times. She would, of course, pay his fees. Her allowance was liberal enough for her to frank some other poor boy in need of aid as well, and the headmaster was even now searching for a likely candidate.

When she came into the bulk of her fortune, she would be able to do considerably more and was even now turning over various plans in her mind. One that she rather fancied was setting up a school for girls, not for daughters of the gentry such as Claire had attended, but a school for very bright poor children, though of course daughters of impoverished gentry who could not pay the school fees would be welcomed, too. And there must be many children of soldiers killed in the war who were in need. The only requirements would be an ability and eagerness to learn. She would need a great deal of advice on how many pupils she could afford to educate and how best to find the type of girls she had in mind.

Perhaps somewhere in the country would be a better place for such an establishment, so maybe she would not settle down in London after all, as she was considering the possibility of running the school herself. It would give her a useful occupation, as it seemed unlikely that she would ever marry.

There had been just a moment at the time she had discovered the truth of her birth and fortune when it seemed as if any fairy tale might come true—even marriage to the handsome prince of her dreams. But time had passed, and that impossible dream was as far from coming true as ever.

Certainly she had met many personable men in London, and some of them she liked very well. Perhaps, had her circumstances been different, she would have entertained thoughts of matrimony with one of them, but she was a woman of independent means, and even should she lose her newfound fortune, no one could take her education from her, so she would still have the ability to make her own way in the world. And that being the case, there was only one reason she would marry, and that was for love.

Unfortunately her heart was already filled by one who did not care for her. There had been a few tremulous moments when it seemed to her as if perhaps he did have some feeling for her, but as time went by, she realized she had been mistaken in that. The wish had been father to the thought. He could obviously never return her feeling. And though she had given herself every opportunity, she could not transfer her own feelings to another.

She thought she must be like her mother, who had loved only once and had not wavered through the years of waiting. However, her mother had had the felicity of knowing her love reciprocated, while such was not true in her own case. She thought it might be more comfortable if she had a different sort of disposition, if she were like a bee who hovered from flower to flower, and if one did not open its sweetness to her she could flit on to the next and the next until she found one which did, and with this she would be content. But it was not so with her, however much she might wish it.

She was no starry-eyed romantic, gazing into the dying fire at bedtime thinking of her beloved's eyes. She was far too practical to sit mooning about, imagining absurd intrigues which would bring him to her side. She had too much zest for life to let herself be moped, so she was very well able to enjoy herself in congenial company. It was just that there was this innermost spot in her heart which was occupied by a tenant who could not be ousted by any other.

Randall Jarvis was often found in Portland Place, and since Iona had confessed the story of their secret betrothal, Jessica could understand why. He came hoping to find Iona there, as indeed was often the case.

On one occasion when Iona was not present, he invited Jessica for a ride in the park, which suited her very well, as the morning was sparkling clear after two days of rain.

As they guided their horses down one of the less-frequented paths, she asked, "How is it that you have time for riding today? You usually have to hurry back to your duties after only a brief call."

"My employer is from town and did not require my services," he said. "He has left me with work to do, but not so much that I can't play truant today."

They talked for a while of political matters, and then he spoke of his hopes of someday acquiring a patron who would put him in the way of receiving a government post, which would be the first step up the ladder. "I am fortunate in that Lord Dumphries has an interest in government, because writing speeches for him and meeting his friends cannot help but put me more in the way of receiving the right sort of attention than if I were merely secretary to some man of property who seldom visited the House. Yes, I am fortunate, though of course there are those who despise me for having to earn my bread by such work. But I am confident you are not one of those, Miss Wyndham."

"Why, no, of course not. As everyone knows, I was once a governess and saw no shame in it. I cannot think anyone who was not very small-minded would despise you, Mr. Jarvis."

"I am glad to hear you say it. And I hope one day to find myself beyond the reach of such small minds. I feel that government service is a challenging ideal."

"Yes, I quite agree."

"Your understanding of political matters has always seemed striking to me. I think you would make a great political hostess if your interests lay in that direction."

She glanced up to find him looking at her in such a particular way that suddenly, without pausing to reflect, she felt compelled to say, "Miss Frayne has confided to me your hopes and hers of a future together."

His eyes changed and at the same moment his horse took a skittish sidewise prance. Mr. Jarvis bent over in his saddle getting the animal under control and gentling it before he turned back to her.

"Has she indeed? I am so glad, for I am sure you will stand her friend—and mine as well, I hope. I am certain you know how much I deplore the need for secrecy."

"Yes, though I wonder if it is any longer necessary now that she is of age. She has convinced herself that her brother still holds the power to cast a rub in the way of your meeting, but I must say he does not seem of so gothic a nature as to keep her locked up."

"I can only defer to her wishes," he said, "for she knows him best. Indeed, I have not been permitted to become well acquainted with him at all." And then after a brooding pause, "Come, shall we put the horses along? This brute of mine is itching for a canter."

She was well pleased to agree, for the conversation made her uncomfortable. In spite of his protestation that he was glad she knew about him and Iona, for just a moment he had not looked glad at all but rather hard-eyed. But perhaps he had only been surprised that Iona would share their secret with an outsider.

It was not many days afterward when Iona came to call. She had sent around a note first asking if she could be private with Jessica that afternoon.

When she arrived, Lady Wellby was in the Red Saloon with Jessica. After twenty minutes or so of conversation Iona said, fixing her friend with a determined look, "And now Jessica, you must take me to your chamber to show me the new gown you were telling me about."

Jessica perceived that this quite mendacious statement was Iona's way of gaining a tête-à-tête, so rather uncomfortably she said, "Will you excuse us, ma'am?"

Joan Stockley was hanging up some freshly pressed garments when they arrived at Jessica's boudoir. She dismissed the abigail, and when the door had closed behind her Iona turned, her eyes bright, almost glittering. "Oh, Jessica, I am so happy. Our plans are all laid. Randall and I are to be married at last!"

"How wonderful! Your brother has given his consent, then?"

"Don't be goosish. He knows nothing of it."

"But Iona—an elopement! You don't want to start married life in such a hole-in-the-corner way."

"It is not precisely an elopement. At least, my family will not know but Randall's will. He has a sister living in Leatherhead and we are to be married there in a church, all very properly—though by special license, of course, because of the banns not being read."

"Your mama will be very distressed, will she not?" Jessica asked.

"I daresay she would have enjoyed the fuss of a big wedding, but she always liked Randall. It was not *she* who has kept us apart. Indeed I once heard her telling Richard he was making a mistake in not allowing Randall to call. I think she will not mind for long once we are actually married, and she is far too good-natured to refuse to receive us."

"But could you not enlist her aid to convince your brother?"

"She can never stand up to him. She is always falling shockingly into debt and appealing to him to pull her out of the River Tick. Besides, there is no time. I know that Lord Griffiths is on the point of making me an offer."

"But you can refuse the offer."

"Oh, yes, but once I refuse I make no doubt Richard will pack me off to the country to think it over.

He could easily enlist Mama's aid. If she decides to close up the house and take me into the country, what could I do? I would be almost wholly at Richard's mercy, and he can make Mama dance to his tune. Being of age is no use at all unless one has money. I could not afford to set up my own house, and I would need a chaperone, too. Oh, sometimes I think being a woman is so tiresome. If I were a man—and had more than pin money—I could hire lodgings and live alone, but I cannot do that. You know I couldn't. Besides, I don't want Lord Griffiths to make me an offer. He— he is really very nice and considerate. I don't want to hurt him. I like him very well, only I cannot be expected to marry to please my brother."

It crossed Jessica's mind that Richard Frayne was a great nodcock. If he hadn't forbidden Iona to receive Mr. Jarvis, if he hadn't pushed her at Lord Griffiths, perhaps all would have turned out differently. She wondered briefly if part of Iona's motivation might not be to thwart her brother. But no, that could not be the whole of it. Perhaps without outside interference, her youthful infatuation for Mr. Jarvis would have worn itself out, but Sir Richard *had* interfered. And now surely that infatuation had deepened into true love, or Iona would not be contemplating such a step. Or perhaps it had been true love all along—as in her parents' case. Who was she to judge the depth of Iona's feelings?

"So you see that we must take action now," Iona said urgently. "And you must help us."

"Help you? How?" Jessica was taken aback.

"That horrid abigail, Laidlaw, whom Richard hired

for me is forever spying upon me and reporting to Richard. I know she is suspicious, and if we can't throw him off the scent all our plans will go for naught, for Richard will find a way to stop me."

"Are you sure you aren't just being romantical?" Jessica asked prosaically. "Sir Richard might disapprove, but I cannot believe he would physically detain you."

"That is only because you don't know him as I do. You see only his company manners. It is so easy for him to convince himself that because he is a man and I am only a female, his opinions are right and must prevail. But why should a woman always have to submit to a man's whims? I do not subscribe to the theory that the mere fact of being a man confers superior judgment."

She could not have found an argument which would have served her in better stead with Jessica. She pushed it further: "If you had heard him say as often as I have, 'You're only a silly girl with no sense and must do as I say,' then you would understand my feelings." She did not mention that it was many years ago when both of them were children that her brother was used to hurl these words at her head. As she was unaware of the fact, the words worked powerfully on Jessica's mind.

"Very well, I will help you," she decided.

Immediately Iona consolidated her gain by saying, "Oh, Jessica, it is so like your parents' case. I only hope they had a friend like you to help them with their plans. Now here is what you must do, and it is very simple really. I will come to see you tomorrow morning in my closed carriage wearing a mantle and come into your house. Then shortly you will come out of the house wearing my mantle and drive away and take the Great North Road. By the greatest good fortune John Coachman is visiting his sick mother, so the undergroom will be driving and I can trust him."

"I really do not see what you are about," Jessica said.

"Don't you see, Laidlaw is suspicious. I could not make all these plans *without* arousing her suspicions. She will be watching me, or have set someone to do it. I'll go bail someone will be watching my carriage at all times, and when it pulls away from here it will be followed. And when it takes the Great North Road, whoever is spying will think I am on my way to Gretna Green. A message will reach my brother and he'll come after it, but it will not matter for you will be in it, while I will be safely on the way to Leatherhead in your carriage."

"But what will I tell him when he catches up with your carriage and finds me?" Jessica asked.

"Tell him you borrowed it. Oh, I know, tell him *you* are eloping. That would be famous."

"Absolutely not," Jessica exclaimed indignantly.

"Well, you may tell him anything you please so long as you don't tell him I have gone to Leatherhead."

"I don't like this very much," Jessica said.

"Well, it would not be necessary if he were not so overbearing and arrogant, thinking he has the right to dictate to me," Iona said. "When I arrive here in Portman Place, I'll be carrying my jewel case and toilet articles done up in a paper parcel. I'll go directly out to the mews, and you will have instructed your coachman to take me wherever I wish to go. When you are safely away, we'll set off. Oh, another thing—I could not afford more than one new gown, but I am having it delivered here to your house this afternoon. But I thought up a famous scheme. I'm having several of my old dresses refurbished. It was the only way I could think of to get them safely out of the house. They will be delivered here, too. Will you be an absolute angel and pack them for me and have them taken to your carriage?"

"But Iona, you surely don't think that once you are actually married, Sir Richard will try to keep your clothing from you! All this plotting can't be necessary."

Iona's face took on a mulish look. "There is no telling *what* he will do when he discovers he has been outwitted by a mere female."

Privately Jessica thought that Iona had allowed her lively imagination to run away with her. All this subterfuge was like something out of a novel. It was in her mind to back out altogether, but then Iona said, "I shall be grateful to you forever for being the instrument of my happiness. And you know—it was the affecting tale of your parents' marriage that gave me the idea."

Jessica felt dismay that she had put such an idea into her friend's head.

"And now that I have convinced Randall and all our plans are made, you *must* help me."

"You *convinced* Randall? He did not wish it, then?"

"Oh, of course he wished to marry me, but he would have had me wait. But when I told him about Lord Griffiths and how if we were not quick I might find myself pushed into his arms, he agreed that this was the only course to take."

And so Jessica allowed herself to be overborne, but when she went to bed that night, her mind was far from easy and she found herself wishing some freak of nature, some torrential storm, would come on the morrow and overset Iona's plans.

She awoke, however, to a sunny day, and she was also somewhat refreshed in her mind. As she was falling asleep, she remembered Iona's words about how her brother was forever telling her she was nothing but a silly girl and had to mind what he told her to do. That was indeed odiously overbearing and made her think that he deserved to be thwarted. She would never have countenanced the runaway marriage of a minor, but Iona was of age, after all, and should be allowed her own choices. And if, because he kept his mother under his thumb, Sir Richard could really force Iona into the country, then, though she personally could not quite *like* subterfuge, perhaps it was the only solution.

Besides, there was the happy example of her parents' marriage to remember. Indeed, by the time she was out of bed, she was fairly well convinced that this adventure would be no bad thing after all.

Chapter Nineteen

The streets of London were behind them, and they had been three-quarters of an hour on the Great North Road bowling through the countryside. In another half-hour or so if Sir Richard had not caught up with her, she would have the carriage brought about and start for home, knowing that Iona had had time enough to make good her escape. Sir Richard would never think of looking in so unlikely a spot as Leatherhead for her, and with all the time he had wasted chasing the wrong carriage, it would be too late for him to stop Iona.

She had in fact begun to wonder if she really were being pursued after all. Suppose it was all Iona's romanticizing that she was being spied upon. Perhaps no one had even missed her. She had sent Laidlaw on an errand before she slipped away, telling the Fraynes' butler that she was going to visit Miss Wyndham. Supposing the maligned abigail were innocent of suspicion and that no one were following her. She fancied that Iona had enjoyed laying her preposterous scheme, but it would suit Jessica just as well if it had been needless, for she did not relish a confrontation with Sir Richard.

She was just at this point in her ruminations when she felt the coach begin to slow. She had heard hoofbeats approaching, but there was a good deal of traffic on the road so there was nothing surprising in hearing a couple of horsemen. But now the carriage came to a standstill and she nerved herself to meet Sir Richard's angry face.

The coach door was wrenched open and to her dismayed astonishment she saw that her apprehender was not Sir Richard but Lord Markham. Of all the unfortunate starts! Had he been sent by Iona's brother? He did not even seem surprised to find her occupying the Frayne carriage.

"May I get in?" he asked with the gravest of faces. "I must talk to you."

Helplessly she acquiesced, but she felt a flush of fury that he should have found her so. She was very much at fault, she acknowledged that to herself, in falling in with Iona's plans, but what right had he—*he* of all people—to come prying? He was forever trying to catch her out in the wrong, it seemed. Well, she would admit to no wrongdoing—not to him. Her chin went up.

He seated himself opposite and looked at her silently with such a look of compassion that she wished herself anywhere but here. Finally he said, "I do not ask what you are doing here, for I know everything. I know you are eloping to meet Randall Jarvis."

She gave a start which he did not seem to notice, opened her mouth to protest, then closed it again. If *that* was what he wished to believe, then let him do so.

"You would be very right to tell me I had no business to interefere," he said, "but I—but you have no brother to protect you. Can you believe that from our long acquaintance, from our having been neighbors, from your having lived in my sister's house, that I am acting as a brother ought in this instance?"

She bit her lip silently.

"I am not condemning your actions; I have not the right; but I believe you are not in full possession of the facts. I believe that you will reconsider this step when you know the truth."

"And that is?" she demanded rather loftily.

"I'm afraid," he said very gently, "that Mr. Jarvis has another interest—another lady whose claim on his affections is . . . considerable."

"I see." She turned her face away to hide a smile. So he knew about Mr. Jarvis and Iona, did he? Well, she would play with him a bit—he deserved it for his unwarranted interference—putting her in such an embarrassing position. "You are sure of this?"

"Very sure," he said steadily.

"How did you know of—of my elopement?"

It was his turn to look away. "I have had my man watching your house—" at her gasp he turned back to her, "since I learned Jarvis had procured a special license. When he saw you leave in Miss Frayne's carriage, he followed until he made sure that your route was the Great North Road. Then he came back to fetch me."

Oh, his presumption surpassed anything! "But why were you watching *me*?"

"It was obvious, wasn't it? Jarvis has been haunting your house, rendering you services, all but living in your pocket. There were other reasons as well."

"Living in my pocket! You are mad. He has come to my house no more frequently than many of my other acquaintance."

"But none of them has taken out a special license," he said.

"If, as you say, he cares for another, then why should he wish to marry me?"

He looked as if he were not going to answer, but then as she leaned forward with the question still in her eyes, he said bitterly, "For the sake of your cursed fortune. He is an ambitious man, you see. It is not unheard of for a penniless man to make his way in politics, but money does grease the wheels. It can buy all sorts of preferments, and an intelligent politician with a rich wife may expect to rise infinitely faster than one without funds. You don't know how often I have wished your money at Jericho!"

She was a little taken aback at his vehemence.

"Oh, of course I could not but be happy knowing you had learned that your parents cared for you. I knew how much it weighed on you, believing you had been deserted by your father. But the money—oh, I wish that Monty Broyles had wasted it all. Only see what grief it has brought already!"

She had been very angry at his assumption that she would consent to an elopement, which was why she had not apprised him of the truth at once. But now he was behaving so strangely. He seemed more sad than condemning. It made her so uncomfortable that she wished to put an end to it. "Tell the driver to turn the carriage," she said. "I will go back."

He dropped his hand briefly over hers. "Good girl."

He told his man to lead his horse; that he would remain in the carriage. She wondered at it a little and considered ordering him out, but his manner puzzled her somehow and she did not do it.

They rode in silence awhile, and then he said, "If you knew in what agony of mind I have found myself over this . . . I've asked myself again and again if I should keep silent, if I only wished to tell you for selfish reasons. As to that I cannot say; I only knew in the end that I could not let you throw yourself away in this manner."

Selfish reasons? What could he mean? Her heart was pounding.

"If I had thought he intended to change, to give her up, I would have said nothing. But she was confident their affair would continue the same as ever. He had promised her that all would continue as before."

She was staring at him in astonishment. "*She?* What on earth are you talking about?"

"Lady Macklin," he said. "She is the—lady in question. She is the estranged wife of a cousin of mine. That is how I came into the affair. My cousin begged me to see her, to plead with her to return to him."

A pulse was racing in Jessica's temple. If Iona were not the other woman Lord Markham had referred to earlier, why then—but this was appalling! She clutched at his sleeve. "Tell me everything at once, and don't try to wrap it up in fine linen," she demanded with blazing eyes.

He was astonished at her sudden urgency and would have denied her the details, but she said, "This is vitally important. Do not spare me. I must know the truth."

"Macklin is a third cousin of mine, much older, who married a beautiful, headstrong young woman," he said. "After a few years she tired of him and formed a liaison with Randall Jarvis. My cousin is a frail and gentle man who lives most of the year in the country. He loves her dearly and could not bear to ruin her or to besmirch his own name with the scandal of divorce. He supports her, and she and Jarvis have been very discreet. I have known of it this age through my cousin, but I think hardly anyone else does. They have great need not to set tongues wagging because of his career, and also because if the affair became general knowledge, perhaps my cousin would no longer scruple to shield her by paying her bills.

"He wrote to me asking that I go to see his wife and beg her to give up this life and return to him. I did, but in vain. She vowed she would never give up Jarvis nor he desert her. 'I trust him so much that even though he is now to marry, things will be the same between us. He has sworn it and I believe him.'

"You may imagine I was surprised at this and said I had not heard of his engagement. 'Oh, there is no engagement. He must run away with his heiress. We have always known he must marry money, but we had hoped to delay for a while. My husband is not a robust man, you know,' she said. 'There was always the possibility I might be freed and with Macklin's fortune. However, there are pressures which make it impossible to wait,' she told me with a strange little shrug. 'He cannot afford to let her slip away. Heiresses are not so easy to come by for a poor man, even one as handsome as Randall, so he has taken out a special license and the thing will be accomplished within a day or two.' I would give much to have spared you this," he finished.

"Spared me! Oh, tell the driver to spring the horses. We must make haste to Leatherhead and pray we are not too late."

He shot her a stupified look but at her prodding did as she bid.

"Oh, we have wasted so much time, and it is all your fault!"

"My fault! I don't understand you."

"How could you have thought I would elope with Randall Jarvis?" she cried in outrage. "Why, I am under age. It would have meant Gretna Green and I would have thus put myself beyond the pale. How can you think me so ramshackle? Was my upbringing not better than that? But you have ever been one to believe the worst of me, accusing me of getting into scrapes which I never did. At least Harry did kidnap me, but that was *not* my fault. Oh, can we go no faster?"

His bewilderment had grown during her outburst. "But if you are not eloping, then where were you going? Why did you—"

"Oh, it was to help Iona elope," she said and immediately added defensively, "and that is quite a different matter because she is of age and has every right to marry where she pleases."

"Iona Frayne is running off with Jarvis?" he said in amazement.

"To Leatherhead. And we must stop her. She knows nothing of Lady Macklin."

"Iona Frayne?" he repeated, his eyes lit with a strange, bright light.

"Oh, do stop saying 'Iona Frayne' in that bird-witted way. Why is it so hard to believe that Iona would run off with Randall Jarvis when you were so quick to believe I would do so?"

"It is hard to believe because I thought the age of miracles was past. And I was not quick to believe you would run off with him. But it had come to my ears some weeks past that he was making too many inquiries about your fortune and how it was circumstanced, so when I was forever finding him in Portman Place playing the gallant—"

"But that was only because it gave him an opportunity to see Iona . . ." she began and then her voice trailed away and she reddened. Or was it? "At least that is what I thought," she went on slowly, "though there was once when—oh, I can't explain, but he—there seemed something in his manner that I would not have expected from a man in love with my friend. I told him at once that Iona had confided their secret betrothal to me and for just an instant I thought he was angry, but then he immediately recovered and said he was glad she had told me. I thought I must have been mistaken about the other."

"I think you were not," he said grimly.

"But why after having already secured Iona's affection, should he have considered me, since it was Lady Macklin he really loved all the time?"

"Because Iona has a brother to look after her interests, whereas you have only Haselipp, Potterby and Haselipp, who might more easily be persuaded to allow a marriage. Because your allowance is far more liberal than Iona's. Because you will come into your money upon your majority, which is only two and a half years away, whereas Iona will not receive hers for four more years. And most important of all, because your fortune is far larger than hers."

"Oh, what a wicked man to use her so shabbily," she cried, and then, "And she told him she was being pressured to marry Lord Griffiths. I suppose that was what Lady Macklin meant by his not being able to let the heiress slip away from him and that was why he agreed to this mad plan."

"If my cousin had died, leaving his fortune to his wife, I make no doubt Jarvis would have married her. She is a bewitching, sensual creature. But the longer the affair went on, the less likely my cousin would be to dispose of his money in that way. So Iona was his trump card held in reserve, but if someone richer should come along in the meantime, such as you, he would have had no scruples in attaching himself to the greater fortune. Only you would have none of it and so he could not afford to lose Iona to Griffiths."

Jessica was fairly sick at the thought of such perfidy. "Can this carriage go no faster?" she cried. "If only you had come to me instead of sending your valet to skulk around!"

"Before you rip up at me further, perhaps you can explain why you lent yourself to such a scheme. Iona has no need to elope, since she is of age."

She bit her lip. "And so I told her, but she is convinced that before he would let her marry Jarvis, Sir Richard would persuade her mother to take her into the country where she could never see Mr. Jarvis at all. And though she is of age, she has not enough money to live on by herself. And since she was determined to have him in the end, it did seem hard that she should have to wait for four more years, and I had told her about my parents, and—and Sir Richard was odiously overbearing, saying she must mind him because she is only a silly girl, and setting the servants to spy on her, and—and—" She was floundering badly, feeling very much in the wrong and knowing that she should never have allowed herself to be persuaded. She wanted nothing so much as to burst into tears, but she could not allow him to see her so missish, so she rounded on him instead. "But you are much to blame. If you believed me about to run off with such a man—as you always believe the worst of me—you should have *told* me about him."

"I hoped you wouldn't allow yourself to be persuaded," he said. "My God, Jessica, don't you think I would have given anything to spare you pain?" There was a raw note in his voice that startled her, and he had used her first name.

The carriage jolted to a stop. The viscount thrust his head out the window. "A cart has overturned in the road," he said a moment later. "They are just clearing it away. I'm going to get out and go the rest of the way on horseback. It will be quicker."

"Very well. Iona said the church is called St. Mary's, and if you don't find them there, Mr. Jarvis's sister is a Mrs. Kirkwick. Her husband is a physician."

She watched as he disappeared down the road. Presently the carriage began to move again. Jessica leaned back against the squabs, a jumble of emotions tormenting her mind.

Foremost, of course, was the terrible worry over Iona. Suppose the marriage had already been performed and they had gone off somewhere together. And then there were the odd things Lord Markham had said. He had been in an agony of mind. He had worried that he might be telling her about Jarvis from selfish reasons. He would have given anything to spare her pain.

Were these the words of a man who saw himself as a brotherly neighbor? But no, she must not let her mind run on so. They had both been overwrought, neither of them heeding their words judiciously. And Iona's safety must be her only concern for the moment. If they were not in time to stop the marriage Jessica would never forgive herself.

Chapter Twenty

The remainder of the journey seemed to take forever, but at last the carriage came to a stop, and looking out, she saw it had been intercepted by the viscount. He leaned in to speak to her.

"The church is deserted—no one around but the verger. He's more than half deaf and I'll go bail a bit of a half-wit. I couldn't get anything out of him except that the vicar is visiting a sick parishioner. I tried to find out if there was a wedding in the church today, but whatever I asked the only answer he gave was, 'As to that I couldn't say.' I came away from the church then, and I have discovered the Kirkwicks' address. I'll lead the way."

He was soon helping her out of the carriage in front of a rather pretty brick house. A boy of seven or eight, very nattily dressed, sat on the steps roughhousing a dog of dubious origin.

"Is this the Kirkwick house?" the viscount inquired.

"It is," the boy said, "but there's no one home but Cook and Milly and they're eating up the cakes and drinking port wine."

"Is Mr. Kirkwick your father?"

The child nodded. "I'm Joshua and my mama won't let anyone call me Josh."

"I'll endeavor not to do so," Lord Markham assured him. "I believe that Mr. Jarvis is your uncle, then. Have you seen him today?"

Joshua nodded, a gleam of mischief in his eye. "Saw him at the church, I did."

"Oh, dear," Jessica exclaimed with a sinking heart. "Was there a strange lady there?"

He nodded. "I was to be *very* nice to her and act a perfect little man because Mama said she'd likely send me presents. I'm much too old to be a perfect little man though, and I shouldn't think she'd send me presents now, but I don't care because *I* thought she was a great wet-goose and very likely the presents would have been something I shouldn't care for."

"Could you tell us what happened at the church?" the viscount asked grimly.

"Well, I had to wear this good suit," he said, smoothing his nankeens, "because I was to see a wedding only it was a mill instead, which I thought was smashing even if it did give Mama spasms."

"There was no wedding?" Jessica cried shakily. "What happened?"

"These two strange gentlemen came to the wedding, only *they* didn't know how to be proper guests because they interrupted the vicar and talked powerfully loud right during the service. One of them said he was her brother, but she wasn't pleased above half when he came to see her get married. And my uncl was mad as fire. Then they went outside and everybody yelled some more and the second gentleman-not the brother—knocked my uncle down. Drew his cork, he did. Then my uncle got up and knocked *him* down. And the lady was shrieking and carrying on, but I thought it was a capital mill. There was lashings of blood and the other gentleman's eye was swelled shut and black as a bat."

"And then what?" his lordship prompted, fascinated.

"Well, that was the end of the fun because they went into the vicar's study, and when they came out the lady was crying like a regular watering pot, and the gentleman with the black eye had his arm around her and she kept squealing, 'Oh, William, I've been such a fool. Oh, William, your poor eye,'" Joshua imitated in a high-pitched voice, "and he was calling her his angel and saying his eye didn't hurt at all and kissing her hand. Enough to make the cat sick, it was."

Jessica burst into weak laughter. "*William!* Somehow Lord Griffiths must have ridden to the rescue along with Sir Richard."

"Yes," the viscount said, "and as it sounds as if they have the matter well in hand, let us withdraw from the area at once and go back to London."

After a solemn good-bye to Joshua as he slipped a sixpence into the boy's hand, he handed Jessica into the carriage and seated himself beside her.

Rather overcome by the alarms of the day, she found herself very cross and said contentiously, "I'm not at all sure it's the thing for you to be riding in a closed carriage with me, my lord."

"A fine time to think of it. You should have had your abigail with you."

"Joan? Oh, she is much too conventional to have taken part in such an adventure."

"But what your abigail finds too shocking is mere commonplace to Miss Wyndham."

She flushed and changed the subject. "Did Lord Griffiths know about Jarvis and Lady Macklin?"

"Yes, he did. I met him as I was coming away from her house the other night. He could see I was troubled and I confided the truth to him, though not my fears for you, of course."

"He must have told the tale to Iona in order to persuade her against the marriage, and Iona must have discovered she cared for Lord Griffiths more than she realized. I always thought she did, but with her brother continually pushing them together, she could not like the idea. Sir Richard has really been very much at fault. If he hadn't forbidden Mr. Jarvis entry to their house and tried to dictate whom she must marry, none of this would have happened."

"Pitching it much too rum, my girl," he said, "trying to push the fault all onto Richard. Are you certain you are not merely trying to find someone else to blame so that your own fault in going along with such a hen-witted scheme will stand out less glaringly?"

Since she was not at all sure but that he was right, she took instant umbrage and went on the attack again. "Well, she was perfectly right about her brother setting the servants to spy on her. She had long suspected it, and the fact that he knew of her plans and followed her today proves it."

"Don't be a nodcock, Jessica," he said. "When she ordered her closed carriage on a warm day like today instead of her phaeton with the announced intention of calling upon you and left the house without her abigail, carrying a large package, and muffled up in an outmoded mantle, the butler would have had to be a perfect looby not to realize that something haveycavey was afoot. I would judge that it was her own flair for the dramatic that gave her away and no intention of Richard's to spy. Naturally a good butler would mention such an odd circumstance to his master. And no one watching your house would be fooled by seeing you take her place, whether you had a hood over your head or not. You're three inches shorter and your walk is nothing like Iona's whatever. In fact I do not see how the brilliant Miss Wyndham failed to perceive at the outset that such a buffle-headed scheme was doomed to failure."

"Oh, you are hateful," she cried, baited until she could stand it no longer. "If you throw in my face one more time the quite erroneous information that I make claims to brilliance, I shall—I shall *hit* you. Indeed, had I known our paths would so often cross I would have taken greatest care from the beginning never to open my mouth but to say, 'Yes, my lord,' and 'No, my lord,' and 'Oh, la, my lord,' and to simper and smirk."

"Which would have made you excessively boring," he said, "and I will say that you are never that. But you are the most exasperating—well, just look at the events of today. If anything could prove that you are still a green girl! Oh, Jessica, who is to guard you from these outrageous scrapes?"

"I haven't given you leave to use my first name," she

said, her heart beating wildly. "And if I get into scrapes, I remind you that it is not your problem. Besides, I shall soon be removed from your vicinity, where you will not be present to witness my many errors and feel obliged to give me the benefit of your superior judgment. I am planning to open a school for indigent girls."

"Good," he said. "Give all your money to the school. That should protect you from fortune hunters, at least."

"I have never stood in the least need of protection from fortune hunters," she retorted. "However, you have missed the point. I am not giving my money to open a school. I intend to run it myself. Mr. Wallace has located a suitable manor house for sale in Yorkshire, which could be made very nicely into a school. The dining hall is some seventy feet—"

"I don't give a damn how long the dining hall is. Who in the devil is Mr. Wallace and who in the devil put such a clunch-brained scheme into your head?"

"Your language is offensive," she said, much on her dignity. "Mr. Wallace is a house agent whom I have consulted. And the idea is my own. It would give a useful direction to my life. One cannot go on attending balls and ridottos forever unless one is completely frippery."

"If that is an animadversion directed at me, you are fair and far out. I am responsible for the running of two sizable estates as well as—"

"Again you mistake me, my lord. I know you work diligently. I was speaking of myself, and as I have no estates to run, I shall run a school instead, as teaching is my profession."

"And bury yourself in the wilds of Yorkshire!"

"Oh, the house is only some thirty miles from York. I daresay we shall be able to arrange expeditions to town so that the girls can see the Minster and the Roman wall."

"Gay to dissipation," he commented drily. "But you will be very much out of the world, alone with a pack of schoolmistresses and pupils. Have you no thought of marriage?"

She seemed surprised. "Why, no, sir; how should I? You yourself seem to believe no one would want me except for my money, and I should not care to marry for such a reason."

"I don't believe that in the least. I only wish you would consign your wretched fortune to the Thames."

"But then how could I start my school?"

"You wouldn't start your school. You would marry and have children of your own."

"But who would marry a penniless girl? It has not taken me a season in London to learn that if a penniless girl is to find a husband, she must be an outstanding beauty or at least have an engaging and conciliating disposition, neither of which virtues I can claim."

"I would agree that you are not conciliating. You are in fact maddeningly perverse. And while you do not have classic beauty, you have something a good deal better, which is countenance. As for an engaging disposition, well, I am bound to disagree with you there, for that is a matter of taste and some people would find you infinitely engaging."

"What a pretty compliment," she said drily. "Well, I have no doubt that with engaging manners, countenance, and maddening perversity I shall do very well with my school. I think that a headmistress need not be too conciliating lest her staff and pupils take advantage."

"You are not going to Yorkshire."

She turned a quizzical glance upon him.

"Oh, Jessica, let me take care of you!"

Her breath caught for a moment but then she said evenly. "I do not need to be taken care of, my lord."

"But it is the dearest wish of my heart to do so. Oh, Jessica, I have loved you so long, since long before I knew it—I think since that day at Gray Gables when you so coolly announced you were going to take charge of your own life, and all the while looking like such a little waif."

There was a little pulse beating wildly in her throat, but she controlled her voice. "If your actions since then have been those of a man in love, then heaven preserve me should your ardor ever cool."

He groaned. "*Maddeningly* perverse. I shall surely strangle you!"

"Ah, another sign of your deep affection, I perceive," she murmured.

"But my actions *have* been those of a man in love—a very stupid man who did not recognize his fate when he met it. And by the time I did, it was too late, for you had that wretched fortune."

"Oh, yes, I quite see that my having money put me quite beneath your touch, despising wealth as you do!"

"It did, Jessica, for if I hadn't declared myself when you were poor, how could I do so when you had suddenly acquired a fortune and the knowledge of a respectable birth? The truth of my feelings burst upon me just as I was on the point of going to my northern estate on some rather urgent business. Fool that I was, I did not come to you at once. I went north and then to Ashendene for Christmas. Then I was coming to tell you, to do my best to win you, only while I was at home I learned of your new circumstance and realized I had left it too late, for how could I ever convince you that I had loved you and wanted to marry you before I learned of it?"

"You might have tried telling me so, my lord," she said mildly, "but then since you never believed my intelligence was of a very powerful order, I daresay you thought I would be too stupid to recognize the truth."

There was a dawning hope in his eyes. "*Would* you have believed me? Can you believe me now? Can you forgive me for not coming to you directly I knew my feelings, and understand that I was a little afraid that when I declared myself, I should receive one of your cool set-downs? Is it possible that you can return my love?"

"Oh, Robert, I think every sensible girl has one silly, impractical fantasy. Ever since I first saw you, riding a great white horse and looking so handsome and elegant, smiling at me and telling me not to be afraid, there has never been the least chance of my loving anyone else. For I believe I have inherited from my mother a fatal inclination to constancy, and not all your subsequent tantrums and boorishness and overbearing rudeness were able to cure me of that early belief in your perfection. However, I warn you that my youthful infatuation will expire of natural causes if you do not stop arguing with me and kiss me instead."

Lord Markham was pleased to comply.

Dell Bestsellers

- [ ] **COMES THE BLIND FURY** by John Saul $2.75 (11428-4)
- [ ] **CLASS REUNION** by Rona Jaffe $2.75 (11408-X)
- [ ] **THE EXILES** by William Stuart Long $2.75 (12369-0)
- [ ] **THE BRONX ZOO** by Sparky Lyle and Peter Golenbock $2.50 (10764-4)
- [ ] **THE PASSING BELLS** by Phillip Rock $2.75 (16837-6)
- [ ] **TO LOVE AGAIN** by Danielle Steel $2.50 (18631-5)
- [ ] **SECOND GENERATION** by Howard Fast $2.75 (17892-4)
- [ ] **EVERGREEN** by Belva Plain $2.75 (13294-0)
- [ ] **CALIFORNIA WOMAN** by Daniel Knapp $2.50 (11035-1)
- [ ] **DAWN WIND** by Christina Savage $2.50 (11792-5)
- [ ] **REGINA'S SONG** by Sharleen Cooper Cohen $2.50 (17414-7)
- [ ] **SABRINA** by Madeleine A. Polland $2.50 (17633-6)
- [ ] **THE ADMIRAL'S DAUGHTER** by Victoria Fyodorova and Haskel Frankel $2.50 (10366-5)
- [ ] **THE LAST DECATHLON** by John Redgate ...$2.50 (14643-7)
- [ ] **THE PETROGRAD CONSIGNMENT** by Owen Sela $2.50 (16885-6)
- [ ] **EXCALIBUR!** by Gil Kane and John Jakes $2.50 (12291-0)
- [ ] **SHOGUN** by James Clavell $2.95 (17800-2)
- [ ] **MY MOTHER, MY SELF** by Nancy Friday $2.50 (15663-7)
- [ ] **THE IMMIGRANTS** by Howard Fast $2.75 (14175-3)

At your local bookstore or use this handy coupon for ordering:

Dell **DELL BOOKS**
P.O. BOX 1000, PINEBROOK, N.J. 07058

Please send me the books I have checked above. I am enclosing $_____
(please add 75¢ per copy to cover postage and handling). Send check or money order—no cash or C.O.D.'s. Please allow up to 8 weeks for shipment.

Mr/Mrs/Miss _____

Address _____

City _____ State/Zip _____

INTRODUCING...

Romantique

The Romance Magazine For The 1980's

Each exciting issue contains a full-length romance novel — the kind of first-love story we all dream about...

PLUS

other wonderful features such as a travelogue to the world's most romantic spots, advice about your romantic problems, a quiz to find the ideal mate for you and much, much more.

ROMANTIQUE: A complete novel of romance, plus a whole world of romantic features.

ROMANTIQUE: Wherever magazines are sold. Or write Romantique Magazine, Dept. C-1, 41 East 42nd Street, New York, N.Y. 10017

Romantique

INTERNATIONALLY DISTRIBUTED BY DELL DISTRIBUTING, INC.

Love—the way you want it!

Candlelight Romances

	TITLE NO.	
☐ A MAN OF HER CHOOSING by Nina Pykare $1.50	#554	(15133-3)
☐ PASSING FANCY by Mary Linn Roby $1.50	#555	(16770-1)
☐ THE DEMON COUNT by Anne Stuart $1.25	#557	(11906-5)
☐ WHERE SHADOWS LINGER by Janis Susan May $1.25	#556	(19777-5)
☐ OMEN FOR LOVE by Esther Boyd $1.25	#552	(16108-8)
☐ MAYBE TOMORROW by Marie Pershing $1.25	#553	(14909-6)
☐ LOVE IN DISGUISE by Nina Pykare $1.50	#548	(15229-1)
☐ THE RUNAWAY HEIRESS by Lillian Cheatham $1.50	#549	(18083-X)
☐ HOME TO THE HIGHLANDS by Jessica Eliot $1.25	#550	(13104-9)
☐ DARK LEGACY by Candace Connell $1.25	#551	(11771-2)
☐ LEGACY OF THE HEART by Lorena McCourtney $1.25	#546	(15645-9)
☐ THE SLEEPING HEIRESS by Phyllis Taylor Pianka $1.50	#543	(17551-8)
☐ DAISY by Jennie Tremaine $1.50	#542	(11683-X)
☐ RING THE BELL SOFTLY by Margaret James $1.25	#545	(17626-3)
☐ GUARDIAN OF INNOCENCE by Judy Boynton $1.25	#544	(11862-X)
☐ THE LONG ENCHANTMENT by Helen Nuelle $1.25	#540	(15407-3)
☐ SECRET LONGINGS by Nancy Kennedy $1.25	#541	(17609-3)

At your local bookstore or use this handy coupon for ordering:

Dell | **DELL BOOKS**
P.O. BOX 1000, PINEBROOK, N.J. 07058

Please send me the books I have checked above. I am enclosing $ _____
(please add 75¢ per copy to cover postage and handling). Send check or money order—no cash or C.O.D.'s. Please allow up to 8 weeks for shipment.

Mr/Mrs/Miss _____

Address _____

City _____ State/Zip _____

MADELEINE A. POLLAND
SABRINA

Beautiful Sabrina was only 15 when her blue eyes first met the dark, dashing gaze of Gerrard Moynihan and she fell madly in love—unaware that she was already promised to the church.

As the Great War and the struggle for independence convulsed all Ireland, Sabrina also did battle. She rose from crushing defeat to shatter the iron bonds of tradition . . . to leap the convent walls and seize love—triumphant, enduring love—in a world that could never be the same.

A Dell Book $2.50 (17633-6)

At your local bookstore or use this handy coupon for ordering:

Dell | **DELL BOOKS** SABRINA $2.50 (17633-6)
P.O. BOX 1000, PINEBROOK, N.J. 07058

Please send me the above title. I am enclosing $_____
(please add 75¢ per copy to cover postage and handling). Send check or money order—no cash or C.O.D.'s. Please allow up to 8 weeks for shipment.

Mr/Mrs/Miss_____

Address_____

City_____ State/Zip_____